MAGNOLIA MILL

Whiskey River Road, Book 6

KELLY MOORE

Edited by
KERRY GENOVA

Illustrated by
DARK WATER COVERS

Magnolia MILL

WHISKEY RIVER ROAD

KELLY MOORE

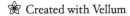

"**D**o you want to make a reservation for next summer before you check out? The rooms fill up quickly." I bat my eyes for effect.

"Aren't you the mayor of Salt Lick? Why are you working the front desk at a bed and breakfast?" The gentleman's wife runs her hand up and down his arm as if I'm trying to steal her man.

"I'm a woman of many talents." Amelia comes tumbling out of Margret's office, walking on her tiptoes. "Where do you think you're going?" I swing her up in my arms.

"A mother, too, I see," the woman says, smiling at her husband.

"Auntie, actually." I place a kiss on Amelia's cheek, and she reciprocates with a big slobbery one of her own. "I prefer this role much better." I don't know why I felt the need to tell her that. In truth, I wish I could have a sweet little girl of my own. *Chin up, Jane. Don't let anyone see your Achilles' heel.*

"I'm so sorry she got away from me," Margret says, rolling her wheelchair out of the office with Chase sitting in her lap.

"I don't mind." I hike her higher on my hip. "Now, how about that reservation for next year?"

"We had a wonderful time. I think we should come back every year," he says to his wife, brushing her hair off her shoulder.

"There will be a ranch option this time next summer. New cabins are being built up on the hill. You'll have the opportunity to sleep under the stars and ride horses all day, along with a meal by campfire every night."

"Sounds great. Sign us up." He grins. They fill out their reservation card and head out.

"Who knew you'd be such a good salesperson?" Margret takes Amelia from me. "You've drummed up so much business for the Magnolia Mill." A glimmer of wetness fills her eyes.

I squat in front of her. "Why the tears?"

"You've sacrificed so much for me. Taking on this place, helping with the twins, and then giving up building on your land to expand the business. All the Calhouns have given us so much."

"Isn't that what families do for one another?" I tweak Chase's little nose. "You look so much like your daddy."

She takes my hand. "I'm indebted to you. I don't think I could've managed after the twins were born without your help."

Chase holds his arms in the air for me to pick him up. "You've given me so much too. I love my niece and nephew."

"They're hardly babies anymore. More like toddlers."

A deep chuckle comes up from behind me. "More like banshees." Wyatt bends down, kissing his wife on the lips. "Hey, darling."

"Howdy yourself, cowboy." She tugs at his beard.

"You smell, Wyatt." I sniff the air, scrunching my nose at the offensive odor.

"One of the cows needed a little help delivering her calf. It was the coolest thing ever. Boone had me reaching up inside the heifer to help her deliver her calf."

"Gross. You need to bathe before you touch the kiddos." I shoo him away.

"She's right." Margret giggles. "You do stink."

He sniffs his armpit. "I don't smell a thing."

"That's because your entire body smells like the inside of a cow, including your nose holes." I pinch my nose.

"Fine. I'll go wash up." He huffs off toward the door. "Boone said Missy and Rose are coming over later to learn how to hook up the horses to the wagon. They're both insisting they want to work at the ranch next summer, so they want a head start."

"Those girls are growing up entirely too fast. Missy is so excited about Moonshine racing in the Derby in a few weeks, I'm surprised she can think about anything else," I say.

"I wish I was going this year, but I'm afraid I've got my hands full with these two," Margret adds.

Ian walks through the grand entrance of the bed and breakfast with five-month-old Deacon in his arms.

"If you smell anything like Wyatt, you need to hand me that baby and go shower." I take Deacon from him.

Ian eases over and sniffs Wyatt. "Damn, man. You smell like...well, I'm not sure, but it smells something awful."

"I've had enough abuse from those two." He points at Margret and me. "I'll be back." He marches off.

"Where's this little angel's momma?" Deacon smiles at me.

"She had to meet someone at the bank to finalize the paperwork on building the cabins." He leans on the check-in counter. "There is still plenty of space left to build you a house down by the river." He picks up a green mint from a shiny white bowl and pops it in his mouth. "I could hire another crew to get it built before next summer."

"I'm in no hurry. I like my room at the Magnolia."

"Oh, sweetie. You don't have to stay here because of me." Margret wheels in front of the counter. "I can manage just fine."

"When I'm ready to build my house, I will. I don't have time to add anything else to my plate. Between my mayoral duties, the property management business I'm setting up with Molly, and helping out here, I'm perfectly content with my living situation." I face her. "Unless you want me to move out? I do have the best room in the inn."

"Don't be silly. You're welcome to live here as long as you want."

"I'd still like to draw blueprints for your house even if it's for future planning." Ian takes Deacon from me.

"I know exactly the style of house I want built. I've known since I was a tiny girl."

Ian stares at me. "Are you going to tell me, or do I have to guess?"

"A castle." I don't crack a smile.

He scowls. "I don't think a castle will fit in with the feel of Salt Lick."

"I'm only teasing." I sock him lightly in the shoulder. "Seriously, I have pictures I can show you."

"Great." He taps the counter with the side of his fist. "Get them to me, and I'll get started on the plans."

Glancing up at the large, rusted clock in the entryway, I turn toward Margret. "I have a meeting I have to go to downtown. There are five more guests checking in today, and only one room left to be cleaned by the maids. I'll come back later and help you make the biscuits for the morning."

"You don't have to do that. I'm good around the kitchen."

"Are you kidding? I wouldn't miss it. You know I love to eat, and you've been teaching me how to cook using all your secret recipes. Speaking of which, Nita said she'd bring pies over later. She knows how much your customers love them."

Ian's at the door, ready to leave with Deacon, who's letting out a big yawn. "I forgot to tell you. Ethan's due back in town tomorrow."

"Okay." I raise a shoulder, not showing any excitement. He's been gone several months helping his mother take care of his dying father. He passed several weeks ago, and he's been packing up his mother and trying to convince her how much she will love living in the country. I'm not as confident as he is. His mother has never been out of the city. I think she's going to have a bit of culture shock. I know this because we've texted back and forth a few times. We quit when things started feeling a little too serious. He wasn't sure if he'd move back here, and I, as usual, don't have time for a relationship, so we cooled it. But I can't deny my insides felt a little quiver at the thought of him returning to Salt Lick.

He's moving his mom to Wyatt and Margret's old place until he can build a house of his own. He says he's nowhere ready to have a ranch, so for now, his land will sit empty.

"I have some ideas for him if he wants to make money off the land." I bite the inside of my cheek.

"I figured you would. I have to put Deacon down for his nap, or he'll be grumpy all afternoon."

"Tell Ellie I'm planning a girls' day out soon." I snag his arm before he can leave.

He grins. "I love when all you Calhoun women go out. Ellie always comes home..." He taps his finger to his chin.

"Horny." I laugh.

He covers Deacon's ears. "Yes. I don't care to know what you ladies discuss, but whatever it is, I get lucky in the end."

"So does Wyatt." Margret snorts.

"Alright. I've heard enough. You two get lucky with your spouses, and I'm stuck with BOB."

Margret giggles.

"Who's Bob?" Ian's brows draw together in confusion.

"Ask Ellie. She'll tell you." I ease him out the door, shutting it behind him. "Men," I say.

"You know when Ellie explains it to him, the next time he sees you, he'll turn pink as Amelia's tiny boots." She holds Amelia's foot in the air.

"Serves him right," I snicker. "I'm going to go change clothes before my meeting. Can I do anything for you?"

"You've done too much already."

I run up the stairs and pull out a light blue knee-length skirt, a silky white blouse, and a pair of black heels. My phone pings as I slide my foot in my shoe.

"Headed home tomorrow. Can I see you?" It's Ethan.

My heart beats faster. I lick my lips before I respond to his text. *"I'll be busy tomorrow in meetings all day."* I hit Send, regretting it. I really want to see him.

"When then?" he sends back.

"*I'm not sure it's a good idea for the two of us to be any more than friends.*"

"*You've mentioned it several times but never tell me why you feel that way.*"

I pause before I answer him. "*Because if we chanced it and it didn't work out between us, we still have to see each other.*"

"*So, you're assuming we won't be good together,*" he responds.

Oh, I know we'd be good together in bed. I've dreamed about it many times. His hands on my body, caressing my nipples, making me wet. Perfection is the only word that comes to mind.

"*Are you still there?*"

"*We come from two different worlds. I'm busy and so are you. I don't have time to commit myself to a relationship.*" Gawd, that sounded cold.

"*Our worlds have come together for a reason, Sunshine. I think we owe it to ourselves to give it a chance.*"

I love it when he calls me Sunshine. "No!" I shout at my phone. I can't. I mean, I won't. My head is on straight, and I've worked hard to get what I want. He'll take time away from me starting my company and my duties as mayor. My finger hovers over the Send button. "*I'm sorry. It's not in the cards for us.*" I tap my bright pink nail on the button, and my heart sinks, knowing I've hurt his feelings.

I see the three dots appear, disappear, and reappear as if he's changed his mind several times about what he wants to say.

"Have it your way," finally lights up my screen.

If I had it my way, he'd be naked in my bed the moment he lands. *"Thank you for respecting my decision."* I'm a flipping idiot. "Gah! What's wrong with me?" I fall back on my bed. Noah would say it's because I'm scared. The only relationship I've ever had ended up with me having a broken heart. If I hadn't gotten sick, my life would be different. We'd be married and maybe have a few babies running around about now. But instead, he left me the minute he found out. Asshole. He said he didn't want to take care of me. "His freaking loss!" I yell. I jump out of bed and walk into the small all-white bathroom to brush my hair. A tear slides down my face as I pull my shoulder-length blond hair into a high ponytail. "I can't ever get married. No man will ever want me when they find out I can't give him a child. Ethan deserves to be a father one day." I swipe away my tear, sticking my chin in the air. I'm okay on my own. I have my career, and sooner or later, I'll have my own home. An empty one, but a home. It's the reason I'm putting off building it.

Living here, I have family, and I get to be Auntie Jane every day. I miss my time with Noah, but Molly and I have truly become sisters. She's the best thing that ever happened to him. He absolutely adores her and she him. She made the most beautiful bride. Noah couldn't quit smiling, and he still hasn't. I wouldn't be surprised if they started a family of their own soon.

All the Calhouns spend a lot more time at the Magnolia Mill Ranch. Wyatt and Margret have made a great home here where they all feel welcome. I think Daddy's had a hard time letting go. He says his house is so quiet now, but he loves that Wyatt has built his own legacy.

I apply one last dash of lip gloss, grab my purse and cell phone, and head off to my meeting. As I fire up my brand spanking new cherry-red Dodge Charger, I laugh, thinking how Daddy tried to talk me into getting a truck. I wanted something fast. Something I could drive like I stole it. The only bad thing is as mayor being stopped for speeding. Mike has yet to write me a ticket, but he's given me several warnings, followed by a stern phone call from Wyatt asking me to please slow down.

Why buy a car like this to drive slowly? I rev the engine and peel out of the Magnolia Mill parking lot.

CHAPTER TWO
ETHAN

"A re you all packed and ready to go, Mother?" I squeeze her shoulders.

"I don't think this is a good idea. My entire life is in this house, in this city." Her eyes gloss over as she sits in Dad's expensive leather recliner.

"I promise if you give it a chance, you'll love the country and the Calhouns. Well, one, in particular, can take some getting used to." I chuckle as I sit across from her on the floral couch she ordered from Paris when she and my father went for a three-month-long vacation a few years back.

"What about my things?" She runs her hand over the beveled glass edge of the coffee table.

"Movers will be coming tomorrow. I've already made all the arrangements. Your things will arrive two weeks from today. Although I'm not sure they'll match the decor."

"What's the house I'm going to be living in like?"

"More like a cottage...the size of your garage."

"Oh my. How will all of my things fit?"

"They won't. We'll have to put most of it in storage until you decide to sell them."

"Sell them?" She's on her feet. "I can't get rid of my belongings."

"They're just things, Mother."

"Ethan Timothy York III! Who are you?" Her brows are scrunched together as her voice rises, making her look older.

"I'm not the same man I was a few years ago. I've learned what's important in life. I never thought in a million years growing up I'd be a cowboy, but there is nothing else I'd rather be."

I stand as she walks over to me, placing her hand on my cheek. "All I've ever really wanted was for you to be happy...but a cowboy?"

"Yes, Mother. There is nothing like mucking a stall, birthing a cow, and wrangling the cattle."

"What about your cybersecurity business with Clem?"

"It's become more of a pastime. My heart is on the ranch. I have a sweet piece of land I want to build on when the time is right. There's so much more for me to learn. But I promise I'll build whatever style house you want on my property."

She turns from me. "I never said this was a permanent move. I only agreed to give it six months. Besides, the money I've made from the sale of this house, I could move to Paris." Her hand toys with the corded gold tassel holding the satin curtains back from the large living room window.

"Do you want to live in Paris by yourself?"

She lifts a shoulder. "You could come with me."

"My life is in Kentucky."

"Is it because of a girl?" Her hand goes on her hip.

"No. Well, yes, because of Clem. You know I moved there with her after we both got out of the military. I had no intention of staying, but I fell in love with Salt Lick and the Calhoun ranch."

"What about her sister? If I recall, you had a thing for her."

"Ellie? She was fun. I was immature, and we've both moved past it. She's married to a great guy, and they have a five-month-old adorable son, Deacon. I work for Ian on the side, helping build homes."

She closes the distance between us. "You've been texting someone. I see your eyes light up when you look at your phone."

"She's a friend, nothing more. She's Clem and

Ellie's sister. You know, I told you about Noah and Jane."

"Ah yes, the twins they didn't know existed. Sounds like Chet Calhoun is nothing but trouble." She sits again.

"I can't argue with your logic, but once you get to really know him, he's not so bad. He loves his family fiercely, and for that, I have great respect for him."

"You like this Jane." It's not a question.

"She's smart, sassy, funny, and pigheaded." I can feel the smile covering my face as I talk about her. I sit, scooting to the edge of my chair. "But she's a Calhoun, and I've sworn off the Calhoun sisters." I'm lying to myself. Ellie was fun, but Jane has inched her way into my heart since the day I laid eyes on her. I regret my infatuation with Ellie, especially if it makes Jane uncomfortable. Something is holding her back from us sharing more than a few flirtatious moments together. I know she has her hands full at the Magnolia Mill helping Margret and her newfound duties as mayor. She and Molly are concocting something together too. I think she puts too much on her plate, so she doesn't have time for love.

"I'd say you protest a little too much. If I've learned anything in my sixty-eight years on this earth, the heart wants what the heart wants. You can deny it, fight it, or walk away from it. But eventually, it will have what it wants."

"You and Dad did love one another, didn't you?"

"We were soul mates," she sniffs. "And now he's gone."

"I'm so sorry, Mother. I miss him too. He was a good dad."

"I don't know what I'm going to do without him," she sobs.

I rise from my chair and kneel in front of her. "You're going to start over somewhere else where every place you look isn't a memory."

"I cherish the memories."

"I know you do, but I don't want them to consume you. If I left you here, you'd make a shrine of his memory throughout this house."

"I'll give it a try. I promise."

"Thank you. That's all I ask." I get up. "I need to check us in to our flight."

"You did purchase first-class tickets, right?" She looks up.

"Of course I did. Only the best for Winifred York." I lean down, kissing her cheek. As I march up the marble stairs to use the computer, I think how much of a culture shock she's going to be in when we get to the ranch. My mother is the sweetest woman in the world, but she's had nothing but the finer things in life. My hope is she'll discover none of those things are important. Clem Calhoun's family did that for me. I'd never go back to this pompous lifestyle.

As I click onto the airline's website, I grab my phone from my pocket. I stare at my last text message with Jane, recalling my mother's words, "the heart wants what the heart wants."

I text, *"Hey, Sunshine. I know you said it's not in the cards for us, but I don't agree. There's a spark between us that needs to be explored not ignored. All I'm asking is for you to acknowledge it. When I get home and get my mother settled, I'd like to take you on a real date. Don't respond now. I'm only putting it out there for you to think about. I'll be home tomorrow."* I hit Send, staring at it as it changes from sent to read.

I log into our flight and check my phone for a response, surprised to see two letters. *"Ok."* I grin like a young boy who paid for his first kiss at the kissing booth with the sweet girl he'd had a crush on for years.

Stripping out of my clothes, I head for a hot shower. Closing my eyes, I envision Jane in here with me. Her blond locks turn dark as the water saturates her hair as she tilts her head back, exposing her long neck. Pebbles of water bounce off her skin as my gaze follows them down her lean body. Her breasts are the perfect size, with small nipples achingly pointing toward my chest. The water continues to bead down her taut belly, dripping into her dime-sized, cute belly button. My hands fit perfectly on her slender hips as my gaze travels further to her bare core. I can see her sweet lips between her legs.

"Damn, Ethan, get ahold of yourself." I shake her out of my head. My cock throbs at my vision of her. "It's not just about how she looks." I talk myself off the edge. "I like everything about her." Maybe she thinks she's too smart for me. She has no idea how I grew up or the education I have behind me. "Of course, she doesn't, you idiot. You've never told her." I don't plan on it either. I've had women all my life throw themselves at me because they saw my family's money. I could give two hoots about being rich. I'd rather be a poor, happy cowboy than a city slicker who thinks his shit don't stink.

Turning off the shower, I push the glass door out of the way, grabbing an overly expensive pale blue towel with our family monogram on it. Wiping the fog from the mirror, I straighten my shoulders. I'm proud of the man I've become. Shaking my wet head of dark hair, water splatters over the mirror and granite counter. I cut my hair before I flew back out of respect for my parents, but I like the longer look on me. My mother has done nothing but fuss about my week-old beard growing in. My father sometimes shaved twice a day to not have a five o'clock shadow. I spent his very last days doing it for him. I loved my father, but we were quite different men. He was always in a suit and polished shoes with his tie flawlessly in place.

His daddy told him it was the only way to be successful in life. Back in his day, I'm sure his words were true. My father met many influential people who helped him garner his success in the technology world. He taught me everything I know, but it wasn't what I loved, like him. He knew it and was okay with whatever choices I made as long as I was an honest man. He stood by me when I told him I wanted to go into the military to find myself. My mother was irate. She didn't understand my need to leave when I had everything laid at my feet.

I wanted to be my own man. It took a while to find myself, but I have no regrets. I've chosen the life I love. The only thing missing is a woman to share it with, and hopefully a family of my own one day. The only person I see sharing my life with brings a smile to my face. Jane.

I dress and head down for dinner. It's the last one we'll have in this house. My mother asked her personal chef to come with us, but he has several high-paying clients in New York that he doesn't want to give up. Actually, I think his nose went in the air at the mention of Kentucky.

Pulling out the chair for my mother, she sits by my father's chair as she's done for years. I take my seat on the other side as the chef plates our food.

"First thing I'll have to do is hire a chef when we make it to the ranch."

I chuckle. "We cook for ourselves, and most of it is food we've grown with our own two hands, not purchased at an expensive supermarket."

"Surely they have stores in Salt Lick." Her mouth drops to the floor.

"They do, but nothing like in the city. Everyone knows everyone, and it's not always about money. We barter for the things we need too."

"Barter? Like in the streets?" Her eyes grow wide.

"No, Mother, with other ranchers and farmers. We help each other out."

Scarlet, my mother's Chinese Crested dog, finds her way to my mother's feet. "Don't listen to him, sweetheart. Momma will make sure you have your fancy food." She pats her head.

"I can buy you a real dog if you'd like." I glare at the thing.

She picks her up in her lap, covering her ears. "She is a real dog," she grumbles.

"I don't know too many dogs running around

wearing pink sweaters with diamonds on the collar." I laugh. "She'll need a winter jacket to cover her furless body." Scar, which my mother hates when I shorten the dog's name, is pure ugly, but she's attached at my mother's hip.

"Don't you worry, my pretty girl. You'll be flying first class with me, and I'll make sure you have your Fiji water." I think the dog juts her chin in the air along with my mother.

"That dog is nothing more than a snack for the hounds running around on the ranch."

"Scarlet will not be allowed around them. I'm sure they have fleas." She scratches the dog's ears.

I love my mother, but this should be fun having her see how the other half lives. I need to ask Chet to go easy on her and hide the dog from him. He's liable to shoot it, thinking it's a rat.

Finishing the food on my plate, I get up. "You should turn in. Our flight leaves early in the morning. Do you need help with any last-minute packing?"

"No, the maid handled all of it for me."

I kiss the top of her head. "Good night, Mother. Your new adventure begins tomorrow."

I walk up the stairs for one of the last times in my life. My father loved this house. Every picture that will be off the walls tomorrow tells a story of his life. Our life. "I'll miss you, Dad," I whisper, touching the gold-framed picture of him. "You were a good, honest man. Thank you for the life you've given me. I promise to take care of my mother. It won't be in the same lifestyle you provided so well for her, but I can swear she'll always be loved and cared for."

CHAPTER THREE
JANE

"We're all in agreement on electing a new livestock agent. Gerald Baker resigned due to his wife's health issues. He requested his son take over, but after a lengthy discussion, he has no interest in taking on additional responsibilities at this time. Do you gentleman have any recommendations?" I study each rancher and businessman sitting around the board room table.

"Boone Methany would be a good agent." Bill Waters leans his denim-clad forearms on the table. He's the oldest sitting councilman in Salt Lick. He was born and raised in this town and knows every man and woman who lives here.

"I couldn't agree more, but he will never give up

his position at Whiskey River." I click the end of my pen.

"Ain't any reason he can't do both," old man Taylor says, as he toys with his gray mustache.

"Don't know unless you ask him." Bob Stanley, who owns the local feed store, touches my arm, and I move it into my lap. He's too touchy-feely for me, and there have been rumors circulating about him having affairs with women who work for him.

"I can put this to bed right now." I dig my cell phone out of my purse and hit Boone's number.

"I'm real busy, so unless it's important, I'll need to call you back." I can make out the sound of horse hooves hitting the ground.

"This will only take a minute."

He tells the horse to whoa, and I hear the leather saddle creak. "You have my attention."

I place the phone on speaker mode. "I'm in a meeting with the city councilmen, and they've requested you take the open position as the new live-stock agent."

"Not interested," he answers quickly.

"Did you hear his response, gentlemen?"

"Boone, this is Bill Waters speaking. Nobody in this town knows cattle like you do. You working as the agent will ensure our association the best prices for all the ranchers. You're the only person that can do the job."

"Thank you for your trust in me, but I'm not interested. I have someone in mind who could be easily trained, and I'd be willing to take on a mentor role for him. He's an honest man with a good head on his shoulders."

"Is it someone from Salt Lick?" Bob asks him.

"Not from here, no. But a man who has come to love this town as much as I do. I wouldn't recommend someone that wasn't right for the job."

"Who do you have in mind?" I ask, piquing my own curiosity.

"Ethan."

"Isn't he the young man that moved in when Clem moved back to town? He was in the military, wasn't he?" Bill points to George, who is a veteran.

"I don't have any more time to discuss it. If you want, we can meet later," Boone responds.

"Thanks for your time." I hang up.

"You know this young man. What do you think?" Bill crosses his arms over his chest.

"If Boone thinks he'd be good at the job, then I'm in agreement." I don't know how Ethan is going to feel about it. I'm a little warm on the inside, thinking he and I would have to work together. "He's due home tomorrow with his mother. His father passed away recently, and he's bringing her back here to live. Once he gets settled, I can ask him if he'd be interested in the position."

"You bring the boy here for an interview so we can see for ourselves." Bill stands.

I push my chair from the table and rise with him. Bob gets to his feet and places his hand on the small of my back. I twist away from him and out of his reach, facing him. "I'd appreciate it if you'd keep your hands to yourself. I don't see you inappropriately touching any of the men around this table. I expect the same."

He lifts his palms in the air. "I meant no harm."

I turn to face the other men in the room. "Are there any other issues we need to address before we adjourn the meeting?"

They glance around the room at one another, shaking their heads.

"Okay. I'll be in touch after I've discussed the position in detail with Ethan York."

Hightailing it out of the office, I head to Molly's building. As soon as I step inside, I peel out of my heels. "Gah, Bob can't keep his hands to himself," I say, plopping down in the wingback chair across from her desk.

"I'm sure you put him in his place." She laughs.

"I feel like I need a bath every time I'm in a room with him." I scrunch my nose.

"I've felt that way many times working with some of my father's goons." She rocks back and forth in her office chair.

"Your father's men weren't good old boys like these men are. I don't know how you dealt with it for so long."

"I got good at faking a lot of things." She glances down as if she's ashamed.

"Hey, don't do that. You did what you had to do to survive. Besides, no more pretending for you."

"Your brother saved me."

"Don't be kidding yourself. You did as much for him. He loves you."

Her face lights up. "I thank God every day for him and for you."

"I'm planning a girls' night out with all the Calhoun women. I want you to come, but be warned, they are a wild crew."

"Really? I can see Ellie getting a little crazy, but not the rest of them."

"Just you wait," I snort. "Are you in?"

"I wouldn't miss it for anything. Name the time and place."

"I'll let you know." I sit up straight. "Do you have the papers you need me to look over?"

She opens a drawer behind her desk and takes out a folder, handing it to me. "It's all there. Take your time looking over the details."

I snag a yellow highlighter out of her pencil holder. "Guess who Boone recommended to the city councilmen for the livestock agent position?"

"I have no idea, but please tell me it isn't my husband. He already works from sunup to sundown."

"Boone thinks Ethan would be good at the job with his mentorship behind him."

She grins. "Your Ethan?"

"He's not my Ethan," I protest, feeling my skin heat up again. I have to learn to control my reaction to him.

"Boone is a smart man. According to Noah, he's been grooming Ethan for a couple of years now."

I stand, pacing the room. "I don't know if it's such a good idea."

"Why, because he'd have to work closely with you for the time being? Might force you to decide how you feel about the man." She taps her nails on the glass desk.

"I don't know what you're talking about. He and I are friends. Nothing more." I stop with my hands on my hips.

"You're only kidding yourself. I've seen the way

you drool over him when you think no one is watching."

"Who wouldn't salivate over him? He's sexy as sin. Doesn't mean I have a thing for him. Any hot-blooded woman would do the same."

"I think you protesting is adorable." She gets up, walking over to me and placing her hands on my shoulders. "What would be the harm of the two of you being together?"

"He's practically family." I roll my eyes.

"Not by blood."

"He had a thing for Ellie."

"And you think he still does?"

"Lord, no. He and Ian are good friends."

"So, your point might be?" She raises an eyebrow.

"I...well...the point is I don't have time for this conversation." I snatch my purse from the chair and pick up my shoes, heading for the door.

"There are plenty of women in this town that would love to be on Ethan's arm. If you don't pay him any attention, he might take one of them up on it. You said so yourself, he's a sexy man."

Noah walks in the door. "Who is my wife calling a sexy man?" He scowls.

"Nothing and nobody. Mind your own damn business!" I press my finger against his shoulder.

"Does this have anything to do with Ethan?" He chuckles.

"Not you too!"

"Do you want to go to the airport with me in the morning to pick him and his mother up?" I see him wink at Molly.

"I have work to do. I don't have time to be a taxi." I swing the door open hard. "Tell him once he gets settled to call me. I have a job offer for him."

Noah's eyes sparkle, and I'm sure some sarcastic comment is rolling around in his thoughts.

"Don't say it." I aim a finger at him. "I'll call you later, Molly," I say, pulling my hair down from its bun and storming off to the diner.

"HEY, JANE," NITA SAYS WHEN SHE SEES ME standing at the counter.

"This place is really doing the business." I glance around to see there isn't an empty seat.

"The guests seem to like the new menu and the chef I hired." She places a clean plastic menu on the counter in front of me.

"I didn't come here to eat, but now that I've seen the size of that burger"—I point to the plate sitting in front of the man next to me—"I'll take two to go. I need to run by the main house. Daddy would love a juicy hamburger."

"I'll have extra bacon piled on Chet's." She tells the chef to pack up two plates. "You said you didn't come to eat."

"I thought I'd save you a trip to the bed and breakfast by picking up the pies."

"I was planning on visiting with Margret and the twins, so it's no problem at all. How is she doing?" She leans down, placing her elbows on the counter.

"She's good most days. She tries to be so independent, and I admire her for it."

"What about Wyatt? He's had a lot of adjustments to make too."

"He adores Margret, and he's such a good father. They really are the perfect couple. Speaking of great couples, I haven't seen Bear much lately, being I don't live on the ranch anymore."

"He's been spending a lot of extra time with Missy. She's been going to Sandy's every other weekend, so when she's home, he's glued to her side."

"How is that going with Sandy being back in the picture?"

"Bear still doesn't completely trust her, and Missy doesn't say much about her, which drives him crazy. She's gone from being a talkative nine-year-old to a closed-lip sixteen-year-old." She laughs. "At least that's how she acts."

"She's a good girl, and she loves those horses. The last time I saw her, all she talked about was Moonshine racing in the Kentucky Derby."

"She says she wants to be a jockey one day. I don't have the heart to tell her she's going to be too tall."

"Boone can teach her how to train instead of ride."

"There are days I feel sorry for Boone. She asks him a million questions, and she's by his side any time he has Moonshine out of the stall. She worships the ground the man walks on."

"Boone's the type man I don't think it bothers him one little bit. He's so good with her and Rose."

"Order up, boss lady." The chef taps the bell.

Nita places the two Styrofoam containers in a white bag with the diner's logo on the side and hands them to me.

I toss cash on the counter. "Keep the change. I'll see you at Margret's later." I turn to walk out.

"I hear you're planning a girls' day," she hollers after me.

"I'll call you with the details as soon as I have them."

CHAPTER FOUR
ETHAN

"How was your flight, Mrs. York?" Noah says as he climbs behind the wheel of his truck.

"Please, call me Winifred." She pats the back of his hand. "It was a good flight." She holds the small kennel on her lap.

"What kind of dog do you have?" Noah tries to look inside.

Mom unzips the lavish carrier and places Scar on her lap.

"What is that?" He points.

"This is my baby, Scarlet." The dog nuzzles its furless body under her chin.

"That is the..." I grasp Noah's shoulder from the back seat.

"Most spoiled pet you will ever meet." I glare at

him in the rearview mirror. I know his next words were going to be, *the ugliest thing he's ever seen.* "Let's stop at the main house first if you don't mind."

"She's not there," he mouths the words.

"Chet has the keys to Wyatt's old place, and I want to introduce him to my mother."

"Are you sure you want him to be the next Calhoun your mother meets?" He chuckles.

"Oh, he certainly can't be as bad as you boys make him out to be." Mother pulls down the visor to look in the mirror and straighten her hair, then turns in Noah's direction. "What is it you do for a living, young man?"

"I'm a foreman on my brother's ranch." I know she wants to grill him with a million questions. "Do you need anything while we are driving through town?"

She looks out the truck window. "This is town? Surely there is more to it."

"No, Mother. We talked about this, remember? It doesn't have all the conveniences of the city. See the café with the red awning?" She turns her head to get a good look. "Bear's wife Nita owns it. Best little restaurant in town."

"Looks like the only one in this place," she says beneath her breath. "Is there a pet store for me to buy Scarlet's food?"

"There's a feed store, ma'am." Noah points to the other side of the road.

"A feed store?" Her voice goes up several octaves.

"You should open your own pampered pet store. You've been wanting something to do to fill your days. I'm sure Noah's wife, Molly, could help you find the perfect location."

"Something to think about." She pets the wiry strands of fur on top of Scar's head. She's quiet as we pass through the rest of town until we meet pastureland.

"The land is green as far as I can see." She stares out the window.

"It's the Kentucky bluegrass. I told you it was beautiful this time of year."

Noah's truck hits a hole as the asphalt changes to a dirt road turning on to Whiskey River.

"Oh dear," she says, holding on tighter to Scar.

"This is all Calhoun property. The cattle on the left, and the horses on the right. The river runs alongside the back of the property as far as you can see."

Noah drives under the ranch sign and parks at the main house. Chet is sitting on the front porch swing, sipping what looks like iced tea. Noah parks, and I hop out, opening the door for my mother. She tucks Scar under her arm and takes my hand. Chet stands as we make it to the top step of the porch.

"Mr. Calhoun, I'd like you to meet my mother, Winifred York."

He rubs his hand down his jeans and holds it out to her. "Nice to meet you, Winnie."

Mother bats her eyes. "Winifred."

Chet laughs. "If you say so."

She shakes his hand, and the dog barks, if that's what you call the noise it made.

"What the hell is that?" He reaches for his shotgun.

"It's her dog," I say, halting his hand.

"That ain't no damn dog. Looks more like a rat."

My mother covers the dog's ears. "I'll have you know she comes from a champion line of Chinese Crested dogs."

"Looks more like a dog with mange."

She gasps. "Mr. Calhoun..."

"Chet," he interrupts.

"Mr. Calhoun," she repeats, "I would appreciate it if you'd keep your opinions to yourself." She huffs.

"No disrespect intended, Winnie, but around here, a dog is for herding cattle and hunting. That thing looks like Henry's snack."

She gasps again. "Who is Henry?"

"He's a goat, and he's only teasing you." I scowl at Chet. Brave, I know.

Chet digs the keys out of his pocket, handing

them to me. "I'm sure Winnie would like to get settled." His eyes have a weird sparkle to them. "Bring her back to the main house for supper tonight. No need to dress all fancy." He grins at her. "Bring your...dog, if you'd like."

"I'm not so sure I want to eat dinner with you." She sticks her chin in the air.

"Oh, get your expensive drawers out of a wad. You're living on my property, and it's the neighborly thing to do."

I stare back and forth between the two of them, waiting to see my mother's response.

"You're right. You've been kind enough to extend your hospitality to me, and according to my son, you mean a lot to him. So, I'll overlook your bad behavior, and we can start over at dinner." She turns on her heels and slowly maneuvers down the steps.

I hear Chet let out a low chuckle. "I like her." He elbows me in the side.

"Then cut her some slack. Be nice," I whisper.

"Boy, when have you ever known me to play nice?" He tucks his fingers in his belt loops.

"Not too often. But do you recall how hard it was for you when Amelia died? She just lost her husband, and she's away from the home and lifestyle she's become accustomed to. Give her some time before you go all shotgun on her." I step to follow her, and he grabs my shoulder.

"I'm sorry, son. Bring her tonight, and I promise to be charming."

"I wouldn't go that far, but thanks."

BOONE IS AT THE RACETRACK, HOLDING THE TIMER as Moonshine trains. "That's a beautiful horse," Mom says.

"If you want, I'll take you to the Derby."

"I'd love that. I have the perfect hat."

I lean over, pointing out the window. "See the cabin behind this house."

She looks. "I know you said the place was small, but..."

"Don't worry. That one's mine." I laugh.

Noah makes his way to the riverside of the property and parks in front of Wyatt's old house.

"Is this it?" she asks.

"Yes. Chet has given me permission to change anything you want inside." I get out and hold her door open.

"It's very cute." I can almost hear her holding back tears.

"It may not be what you're used to, but I promise if you give it a chance, you're going to love it here."

She tucks her bottom lip between her teeth to hold back her emotions. "I promise to try."

"Good, that's all I ask."

Noah takes her luggage out of the bed of the truck and hauls it inside. "I'll put this in the master suite." He disappears for a moment then comes back into the room. "It was very nice to meet you, Mrs. York. Molly and I will have you over for dinner one night, but I'm afraid I have work to do."

"It was nice to meet you too. Thank you for picking us up at the airport." Mom holds her hand out with her fingers facing down. Noah looks at it awkwardly, then shakes her hand. "Let me know if there's anything we can do to make you more comfortable." He tilts his hat and walks out the door.

"This old couch will be gone when your furniture arrives. I borrowed it from another cabin, so you'd have something to sit on. Margret bought new beds for the bed and breakfast and said you could use one of them until yours arrives from New York."

"That was extremely sweet of her. You don't have to fuss over me. I'll be just fine."

"I'm going to let you look around and unpack. I'll take you into town tomorrow to get supplies. We can pick out paint if you'd like, and I can have one of the men slap it on the walls for you."

"It's been a long day already. I think I'll unpack my suitcase and lay down for a nap after I take Scarlet for a walk."

"Why don't you let me do that before I leave."

She takes a pink studded leash out of her over-sized purse and snaps it to her collar. If any of the Calhouns see me, I will lose my man card. Cowboys don't walk froufrou dogs on a leash. Especially ones with matching pink ribbons in their hair. *I love my mother. I love my mother.* I keep repeating this mantra under my breath.

The dog acts as if she's never walked in real grass before. She slowly picks up each paw, and it looks as if she's prancing.

A dust of smoke rises as I hear the four-wheeler come to a stop. Bear pulls down his bandanna from his face. "Is that supposed to be a dog or what?" He comes stomping toward me.

"Keep your voice down. My mother may hear you, and she's already had to deal with the likes of Chet teasing her about it."

"I'm betting it was brutal," he snorts.

"They didn't get off to the greatest start."

"Daddy never makes the best first impression."

He squats to get a better look at Scar. "Sure ain't purdy. I'm guessing the girls will love her."

"Do you think Missy and Rose could have dinner at their grandpa's tonight? My mom could use the buffer."

"I'll see to it." He stands. "I saw Noah's truck leaving and figured you were back. Welcome home. We've missed you around here."

"Thanks, man. It's good to be home."

"Boone was out at the track and said he needed to talk to you about something."

I glance at my watch. "Can it wait?"

"You itching to see Jane?" he snickers.

"I am, but I don't think the feeling is mutual."

"She's at the Magnolia Mill this time of morning helping Margret with the customers."

"She said she'd been lending a hand."

"Jane's practically running the place. I think it's filled a need in her to help. She said she's paying it forward for all the assistance she received when she was ill. Besides, she loves being around the twins."

"I bet they've gotten big since I've been gone."

"They both started walking not too long ago. Won't be much longer, and Deacon will be on their heels."

"I'll have to stop by and see him. He was only days old when I left for New York."

He places a hand on my shoulder. "I'm sorry about your father."

"Thanks. The last month was hard, watching him waste away and be in so much pain. He's better off now."

"How's your mother handling it?"

"She misses him, but she'll be alright. I'll see to it."

I walk him to the ATV. "You ready to start back to work in the morning?"

"Yeah, I'll be there. Maybe I could convince Nita to take my mom into town to get a few things tomorrow."

"She'd be glad to help. I'll have the girls at Daddy's by seven."

"Thanks." He rides off, and I hop in my pickup, headed straight for the Magnolia Inn.

The parking lot is full of guests coming and going. I hold the large wooden door open for a couple leaving with their suitcases being rolled behind them. The first person I see is Jane behind the check-in counter. She has her pretty blond hair braided to the side. A wisp of hair falls in her face, and she sweeps it behind her ear. Her soft pink blouse matches the color of her shiny lips. Her baby blues find my dark eyes, and I see her swallow.

"Busy place," I say, sauntering up to her.

"You're back." Her eyes twinkle as a smile pulls on the corners of her gorgeous lips.

"I thought I heard your voice." Margret wheels out of her office with the twins in her lap. "Come give me a hug." She holds her arms in the air.

I bend down to embrace her.

"We've missed you around here," she says. Then she whispers, "Especially that one and don't let her convince you otherwise."

I grin. "It's good to be back." I pick up Chase. "What have you been feeding these two? You sure look like your daddy." Chase smiles, and I see his two front teeth. I reach down and tweak Amelia's cheek, and she squeals. "What a beauty," I say.

"This one's a handful," Margret responds.

I glance over at Jane, and she has a strange look on her face. The smile she was sporting is gone. "You okay?"

"Yeah, yeah, I'm fine." She looks down, flipping through the registration book. "We have two more couples checking out this morning and two more due in this afternoon."

"Do you have time to grab a cup of coffee with me?"

"Sure she does. I can handle this." Margret shoos her away from the desk.

I follow Jane to the kitchen. "Your flight arrived early. Did you eat?"

"Not since the dry bagel I had at the airport at five this morning."

"There is leftover ham and biscuits if you're hungry."

"I'd love some."

"Where's your mom?"

"At the ranch, napping."

"Do you think she's going to like it here?" She opens the fridge, taking out the leftovers.

"I hope so."

"Have you spoken with Boone yet?"

"No, but I heard he wanted to talk to me. What's it about?"

"The councilmen want to interview you for the livestock agent position that has come open. Boone recommended you for it."

"Livestock agent?" I sit on the barstool as she warms the food.

"He thinks you'd be the perfect man for the job."

"I might be interested. I've been wanting something more to do."

"You're not a shoo-in. They will want to interview you." The microwave dings and she places the plate in front of me. "I know you have mad computer skills and that you've been in the military. Do you have a college education?"

I take a bite of food. "I do. When I graduated high school, I had my two-year degree in my hand. While I was in the service, I finished my next two years."

"What did you major in?" She hands me a coffee, and she sips on lemonade.

"Besides computer technology, I have a math degree."

"You were a geek?" She giggles.

"The geek becomes the cowboy." I laugh.

"Wow, there's more to you than meets the eye, isn't there?"

I lay my fork next to my plate and rub my hands down my jeans. "I want us to go on a real date." She opens her mouth to say something, but I stop her, holding up my hand. "Hear me out. You can deny it all you want, but there has been something building between the two of us for a while now. I think we should explore it."

She walks over to the white porcelain oversized sink and pours what's remaining in her glass down the sink. "I don't think it's a good idea."

"Why not? And don't give me this we come from two different worlds." I stand, closing the gap between us.

"Because, if it doesn't work out, we still have to see each other."

She closes her eyes, and I get so close to her face I can almost taste her. "And if we do work out, think how good it could be," I whisper.

Her eyes pop open, and her breath hitches. I lean in and softly kiss her lips.

"Ethan," she rasps.

"Say you'll go out with me." I pin her in with my arms as my mouth explores her neck. "I've wanted to kiss you since we danced in the bar. You taste sweet, just like I imagined."

"Alright, you win." She places her hands on my chest and pushes me away. "We can go out, but I'm not making any promises."

My face feels as if it might crack from the smile on it. "I'll pick you up tomorrow at eight. Wear something soft and pretty, not your business attire," I say, backing out of the room.

CHAPTER FIVE

"Don't you two look mighty purdy tonight." Missy and Rose have on what looks like Easter dresses.

Missy twirls around. "Sandy bought it for me, and Rose begged Uncle Boone for a matching one."

"They're awful fancy for a dinner at my house. It's spaghetti night." I hand both of them one of Amelia's old aprons to put on.

"Did you use Grandma's recipe for the meatballs?" Missy takes the lid off the pot on the stove.

"I sure did. Do you young ladies want to finish making the salad?" I give Rose a set of tongs.

Ethan comes into the kitchen with his mother on his arm, and that thing she calls a dog tucked under hers.

"Oh my gosh!" Missy squeals. "She's so cute!" She runs over to the mutt.

"Missy, Rose, this is my mother," Ethan introduces her.

"It's so nice to meet you. Can I hold her?" Missy asks all in one breath.

"Certainly, but be very careful with her. Her name is Scarlet." She hands the thing to her.

I take a minute to look at Winifred. She's attractive with a touch of silver in her dark hair. I bet in her day, she was downright purdy. She looks like an expensive bottle of perfume from where I stand. The high-maintenance kinda stuff. That was the one thing I always appreciated about my Amelia. She was happy without the finer things in life. I would've given them to her if she wanted them, but she didn't.

"I have iced tea or lemonade. Which would you prefer?" I ask her.

"Do you have any whiskey?"

Ethan's eyes grow in surprise at her response. "You want whiskey?"

"You've come to the right place. Look in that cabinet over there and take your pick." I point.

She strolls over and opens it up. She takes a bottle down. "This was my husband's favorite," she says, then places it back on the shelf. "But this one is mine."

I walk over and take it from her. "American whiskey. Good choice. Straight up or on the rocks?"

"Two rocks," she answers.

A woman that knows what she wants. There ain't nothing wrong with that.

"Can I have one too," Rose asks.

"Not a chance." I chuckle.

"Oh, Grandpa. I've tasted it before. I snuck a sip of Daddy's when he wasn't looking." Rose stands like Clem does when she's getting all uppity about something.

"He'd tan your hide if he knew."

"You ain't gonna tell him, are you?" She pouts.

"Not if you promise to not do it again." I watch her cross her fingers behind her back and make a mental note to give Boone a heads-up about his whiskey-tasting ten-year-old.

"Momma Sandy has let me drink her beer," Missy chimes in.

"She ain't supposed to be drinking anymore." I give her a sour look.

"It's just beer." She shrugs.

"Let's talk about this another time." I take down three glasses and place two balls of ice in each one. I hand one to Ethan and the other to his mother. "Here's to new friends." I raise my glass.

"I could use a friend or two," she says, lifting hers.

I drink mine all at once and set my glass on the counter. "Boone was looking for you." I eye Ethan.

"I ran out of time, but Jane told me he wants to talk to me about the livestock position."

"What are your thoughts on it?"

"I want to weigh all the options and do some research, but I think I'd like the opportunity to interview for it. If Boone is willing to give me some pointers, I think I'd do well."

"Boone has been bringing you along since the day you moved here. He tells me you're smart as a whip with numbers and the computer. I'm sure you'd do fine."

"Of course, he would," his mother chimes in. "I don't know what a livestock agent is, but my boy can do anything he puts his mind to. He graduated at the top of his class. I'm just not sure why he'd want to waste all his talents being a cowboy." She sips her whiskey.

I jut my chest out. "Nothing wrong with being a cowboy or a rancher. Do you think this land and all the cattle take care of itself? It's a business like anything else. Takes brains and brawn to run it."

"I meant no disrespect, Mr. Calhoun. I only thought he'd be running a tech company like my husband."

"Please stop with the formalities. Call me Chet." I

turn off the boiling noodles. "When I first met your son, I'd say I agreed with your assumption." I pour the noodles into the strainer sitting in the sink. "I learned quickly the boy had both brains and guts. He took a likin' to the ranch, especially the cattle. With his knowledge of numbers and his acquisition of live-stock for this ranch last year, he'll be what this town needs to help the ranchers in Salt Lick to get the best deals for their stock."

By the look on his face, I can tell Ethan had no idea what I thought about him. "Thank you, sir." His voice is choked.

I walk over to him. "You've become a son to me just like Boone."

He has that glassy look like he could shed a few tears. "That means a lot to me."

"Enough of this mushy stuff. Girls, put the dog down and go wash your hands. Supper is ready." I toss a dish towel over my shoulder.

Winnie walks over to the sink and helps the girls, then washes her hands too.

I put the food on the table, and the girls sit. My heart aches a bit when Winnie sits in Amelia's chair. Ethan moves toward her, but I stop him by lifting my hand. "It's about damn time someone sat in that chair." My voice cracks.

Winnie starts to stand, but I place my hand gently

on her shoulder. "I'm sorry. Is this your wife's seat?" she asks.

"Yes, and she'd be glad you're sittin' in it." I take the chair next to her.

"You're so purdy," Missy says, handing her the pasta.

"Why, thank you," she responds.

"Do you think I could bring Scarlet home with me?" She looks down at the dog sitting at Winnie's feet.

"Maybe after she's adjusted for a few days. How about you come over, and you can play with her at my house?"

"Do you have different clothes to dress her up in?"

"She ain't a Barbie. She's a dog." I laugh.

Winnie ignores me. "Yes, she's got several outfits for you to choose from."

Ethan squints at me and chuckles under his breath.

"I hear you love horses, and one of them is going to race in the Kentucky Derby," Winnie says to Missy.

"Moonshine. He's going to win too." Missy's eyes light up like a Christmas tree. "Uncle Boone's been training him, and he's the best!"

"My son has graciously offered to take me to the races. Do you have a pretty hat picked out to wear?"

"No. Not yet." Missy takes a mouthful of spaghetti.

"I'd love to purchase dresses and hats for the both of you to wear," she tells the girls.

"My mother loves to spend money," Ethan states. "Knowing her, she'll order them something from Paris. I'll get a computer in your house tomorrow and make sure the internet is hooked up."

"Can I have a pink one? Pink's my favorite color," Missy squeals.

"You can have any color you want. How about you, Rose?"

She taps her finger to her lip. "I think yellow would be pretty."

"Yellow it is." Winnie smiles.

"Winnie, would you like some more whiskey?" I stand to pour Ethan another drink.

I wait for her to correct me on her name, and I'm surprised when she doesn't. "I'd love another one." She holds up her glass for me to refill.

CHAPTER SIX
JANE

"I'm so glad we are doing this. I know I'm part of the family, but it's nice to have a girls' night out." Molly closes the door to her Mercedes.

"I thought it'd be nice to support a new local business, and the Calhoun women are going to love this." We stop and read the logo on the large front window.

"The Paint and Pour," Molly says.

"Who wouldn't love painting and drinking wine at the same time." I giggle.

She holds open the door, and we walk inside. Clem, Ellie, Nita, and Margret are already inside, sitting in the back row of chairs with easels in front of them.

Clem stands, hugging me. "I love this place."

"So do I." Ellie holds up a glass of red wine.

"This is going to be so much fun." Margret picks up a paintbrush from a cup sitting by her palette.

"Before we start our girls' night, there is one rule."

"Rules?" Ellie cocks her head.

"Yes. We never make it through one of these evenings without each of you leaving to go home and have sex with your husbands." I point to each of them.

"Really?" Molly smiles. "I knew I liked you ladies."

I move around to the front of the table to face them, propping a stern hand on my hip. "No pictures of your titties to your husband." I glare at Ellie, and she smirks. I pick up the container beside Clem. "This Saran Wrap is for the brushes, not some kind of kink with Boone." Clem turns the color of red paint.

Molly leans over to her. "Do tell. I haven't heard this story."

"Margret, Wyatt is manning the bed and breakfast, so no distracting him."

She sweeps a strand of hair from her face. "He's not *hard* to distract." The others burst out laughing.

"Don't be mentioning *hard*." Nita slaps her leg.

"And you." I square my body toward Nita. "Don't be running over to the bar. Bear is entertaining the townsfolk tonight."

I march back around the table and sit by Molly.

"We're here to have fun together. Forget your men tonight."

Ellie inches toward Clem and mutters, "She needs to get laid."

She moves forward to look at me. "Speaking of which, where's Ethan tonight?"

"I'm not screwing Ethan," I say with pursed lips.

"Well, why the hell not?" Margret puts in her two cents.

"Leave her alone," Clem snorts.

I righten myself in front of my easel, tugging down my white blouse. "Just mind your own business," I snarl.

"Margret's right. Why aren't you sleeping with Ethan? He's hot," Molly says.

My face springs in her direction. "Not you too!"

"I happen to know he's at the bar, listening to Bear's band." Nita pulls a white apron over her head.

"I thought he was helping his mother watch Missy and Rose," I say.

"Wyatt said all the kiddos ended up at the main house. Chet and Ethan's mom are babysitting the whole brood of them."

"I think Daddy likes her," Clem chimes in.

"Who?" I frown.

"Who do you think. Ethan's mom," Ellie howls.

"They've only just met," I retort.

"Don't matter. Ethan says he was nice to her, other than that thing she calls a dog," Nita adds.

"Daddy ain't nice to anyone he don't like," Clem points out.

The lady who owns the Paint and Pour clears her throat. "Thank you for signing up to paint tonight. There's plenty of wine. A server will come around while you're painting to fill or refill your glasses. It appears some of you have already helped yourself." She glances in Ellie's direction.

"Cheers," Ellie yells.

Penny, according to her fancy name tag, angles herself toward a painting beside her. "This is what we'll be creating tonight on canvas." It's a picture of a horse in a pasture underneath a full moon.

"That looks like the view outside my window every night," Ellie snarks.

"Once you get the basics down, you can give it your own flare." Penny shows us another painting of the same picture but with tall trees added in.

"I'm going to give it my own flare alright," Ellie mutters under her breath.

"Your artistic instructor tonight is Sera. She'll demonstrate how to get started, and I'll come around giving out pointers." Penny slips a red apron over her floral dress, tying it in the back. "Each of you has an apron to protect your clothes from paint spills."

"How about that refill of wine." Ellie holds an empty stemless wineglass in the air. Another lady comes over, filling each of our glasses. "You can leave the bottle." Ellie frees it from her hand.

Sera starts talking, and we mimic what she's doing on canvas. Penny walks to the first row of people, helping them out. She makes her way to our row and stops by me.

"Aren't you friends with Ethan?" His name slides from her lips, causing an instant dislike for her.

"We're all friends with Ethan." I sit taller, holding my paintbrush still on the canvas.

"I've seen him in the diner a few times. Is he currently involved with someone?" She bats her dark eyes.

"No. He's a single man," I respond curtly.

All sets of eyes in the back row are staring at me.

"He's a fine-looking cowboy. Maybe one of you ladies could introduce me."

"She's mistaken. Ethan is taken." Clem scowls at me.

"Well, if he don't have a ring on his finger, he's still a free man," she says, moving back to the front of the room.

"I don't like her," Molly whispers.

"Ignore her. We came here for a good time." I continue to slap paint on the canvas.

Our glasses of wine are refilled several times, emptying three bottles of wine. My background looks good, but my horse is a little wonky. I'm leaning in, trying to fix it, when I hear Clem gut-laughing.

"That is definitely not a horse!"

I scoot my chair back to look at Ellie's painting.

"Oh my." Margret covers her mouth with her hand.

Nita is holding her stomach, giggling.

Molly's eyes grow wide. "Is that..." She can't finish her sentence.

"I don't think that's a horse," I say, trying to hide my amusement.

"Sure, it is. It's Ian's horse," she says, raising a shoulder. "She said we could add our own flare."

"I think she meant with different colors, not your husband's manhood painted all over the canvas."

"She's one lucky lady," Molly snickers.

"Is that really his whippersnapper?" Clem stands behind Ellie, looking at the painting.

"Yep, I have a picture of it right here." She holds her phone up to Clem, and she covers her eyes.

"Why do you have a dick pic from your husband on your phone?"

Ellie angles her head up to look at Clem. "A better question is, why don't you have one from Boone."

"Even if I did, I wouldn't broadcast it to you."

She snatches Clem's phone that was lying beside her painting. "You do have one, don't you?" Clem fights to get it back from her.

The other row of women have turned in their chairs to look at us. Some are giggling; others are sneering.

Penny storms toward Ellie to see what all the laughing is about. When she glances at Ellie's artwork, she gasps. "This is most certainly not what I meant about creative flare."

"Well, it should be. We live on a ranch, and you want us to paint pictures of horses. This is much more interesting." Ellie crosses her arms.

"I think you should leave." Penny points to the front door.

Ellie picks up her glass of wine, taking a sip and ignoring her glare.

Penny directs everyone's attention back to Sera.

"She's right. It's time to go," Ellie says.

"You've snapped a picture and sent it to Ian, didn't you?" Margret giggles.

"He'll be here in five minutes to pick me up." Ellie stands, removing her apron.

"Do you not remember the only rule this evening?" I glare at her.

"Rules *smooles*." She waves me off. "You told me I couldn't send pictures of my titties. You said nothing about me snapping a painted picture of my husband's junk. I think you need to be a little more specific next time." She takes her picture off the easel and heads out the door.

I hear Clem and Margret whispering, knowing damn good and well they are up to something.

"Oh, look at the time." Margret lifts her wrist. "I have to get up early in the morning with the twins."

"Aren't they all spending the night at Chet's tonight?" I stare at her.

"Still, he'll want me to pick them up as early as possible." She wheels back from the table.

"It's only eight," Molly states.

When Margret rolls behind her, she says, "That gives Wyatt and I plenty of alone time."

"I have to drive her home." Clem takes down her picture and Margret's.

About that time, I peer out the front window, seeing Wyatt's big ole truck pull up.

"You've texted Boone, haven't you?" I laugh.

She snatches the container of Saran Wrap. "You have no idea the things you can do with this." She holds the door open for Margret.

Nita tries to slip out without me seeing. "Where are you going?"

"Bear has a ten-minute break." She lifts a shoulder, grinning from ear to ear.

I splash some color on my canvas. "Looks like it's just you and me," I say to Molly. When I glance in her direction, she's turned toward the back of the room, taking a selfie with her blouse unbuttoned.

"Not you too!" I snort.

"If you can't beat 'em, join 'em." She clicks send. "Do you think you could hitch a ride home?" she asks, standing. "This was so much fun. We'll have to do it again soon." She grabs her painting.

Why did I bother? I knew exactly how this night would end. Problem is, I'm jealous. "I'll be fine. Don't worry about me," I holler as the door closes behind her.

I sit alone in the back row, sipping my wine and finish putting the last touch of color on the dark sky in my painting. Tossing my brushes in a plastic container of water, I tug off my apron to leave. Penny meets me at the door.

"I think you Calhoun women should find something else to do on a Friday night in this town." She taps a long red nail to her chin. "That is unless you want to bring Ethan to one of my classes."

Jealously bites in my gut. "With a man like Ethan, painting is the last thing he has on his mind. He's probably got some hot redhead's legs parted as we speak." I hold in my laughter at the look on her face. I leave with my canvas gripped in my hand. I storm toward the bar a block down. If Nita and Bear are done, she'll give me a ride home.

There's not an empty spot in the parking lot. This is the most popular place in Salt Lick. Especially when it's Bear's night to entertain. I don't know how Nita tolerates all the women who throw themselves at him. She seems to take it in stride, knowing he's coming home to her.

I push my way through the crowded bar, looking for Nita. There is no sign of her. The jukebox is playing, so I'm assuming their ten minutes isn't over yet.

I find a small inch of counter to lean on at the bar. The bartender places a small square napkin in front of me. "What will you have?"

"Diet Coke, please."

He grins. "Big drinker, huh." He reaches under the counter and pulls out a short glass, filling it with soda and then places a lime wedge on the edge.

"I thought the Calhoun women were out on the town for the evening." From behind me, a familiar voice—not to mention too much wine in my belly— makes my insides tingle.

I turn to see Ethan. Why does he have to look so damn good? "It ended in its usual fashion. The Calhoun men and women seem to be very horny." I laugh.

He moseys closer to me. "Ain't nothing wrong

with that." His voice is so sexy I have to squeeze my thighs together. "You look pretty." His gaze is filled with appreciation as it scans my body.

"Penny at the Paint and Pour wants to meet you," I say, as a distraction to my thumping heart.

He leans in closer, twirling a piece of my blond hair between his fingers. "I ain't interested in Penny. You agreed to go out with me the other night and canceled. What are you afraid of, Jane?"

His breath bounces off the nape of my neck. "You," I whisper.

He stands tall, straightening his spine. I see his jaw flex back and forth, glaring at me. "I'm going to wash the fear right out of your head." He takes my hand, leading me through the crowd and out of the bar.

CHAPTER SEVEN
ETHAN

"I'm sorry I canceled on you the other night," she says before I shut the passenger side door. I can feel her watching me as I scramble around the front to climb behind the wheel.

"You'll make it up to me tonight." I don't look at her.

"Where are you taking me?" I reach over, fastening her seat belt. She tosses her painting over the seat.

"Home." I put my arm on the back of the seat, looking over my shoulder and backing out of the parking lot.

"That's not a date." I feel her glare in the dark.

"You had your chance at a romantic night out. Now we're going to do things my way." My voice is deep and raspy.

She gulps, more than likely having no idea what that really means. "You could take me to the Magnolia Mill, and we could plan another date." I hear the questioning in her soft voice.

"I don't trust you to keep your word." The truck bounces over the uneven road.

"You're taking me captive?" Her voice goes up several octaves.

"Call it what you want. You and I have been dancing around each other for the past year. It's time we put a stop to it."

"I kinda like the dance we've been doing," she mutters.

"You mean the one keeping me at arm's length?" I glance in her direction, and she slightly lifts a shoulder.

I'm done playing games with her, and I no longer care that she's a Calhoun woman. Every part of me wants her, and I'm tired of holding back. I was so mad at her the other day for texting me to call off our date I could've spit. I had every intention of giving her what-for until I saw her in the bar tonight by herself. She was oblivious to all the men watching her. She can be intimating at times, so not many men approach her. They don't see the softer side of her like I have; it's rare, but it's a beautiful thing. Keeping my eyes glued to the dark road, in my peripheral, I see her gnawing on the inside of her cheek, and her left leg is nervously bouncing up and down.

I take my hand off the steering wheel and place it on her thigh. "Hey, it's not like I'm going to force you to do anything you don't want to."

The corners of her lips turn to a smile. "I know. I'm not afraid of you, per se."

"What then?"

"It's hard to put into words."

"When you're ready, I'm listening." I place my hand back on the wheel to turn down the dirt road to Whiskey River.

She's quiet as we pass the main house to the east side of the property. The outside light at Ellie and Ian's is on as I turn the corner to my small cabin.

As I shift into park, Jane jumps out before I'm able to jump out to open her door. I click the remote, locking my truck. Unlocking the front door, I flip on a light.

"When are you building on your property?" she asks, taking a seat on the two-seater couch.

"When the time is right. Can I get you something to drink?"

"Water would be appreciated."

As I'm fixing her a glass, I flip through my phone, connecting with the speakers in my house and turning on music from the eighties. Walking over to her, I hand her the water.

"Thank you," she says, taking it from me, sipping it, then setting it on a coaster on the coffee table.

"Would you like to dance?" I hold my hand out.

"Here?" She points downward.

"It's a date, remember. This is what people do in this town when they're on a date."

She stands. Handing her the glass, I move the coffee table out of the way and then set her water back down. Facing her, I hold my arms out. She hesitantly puts one hand in mine and the other on my shoulder.

The corner of my mouth lifts to a grin. "You look beautiful."

She snuggles into my shoulder, and our bodies sway together to the music. "This is nice," she says.

"*Nice*," I repeat the word back to her.

"Do you have something against nice?" She laughs.

"No, but I'd like something more between us than *nice*."

She leans back to stare at me. "What is it you want from me, Ethan?"

"I want it all."

"How can you say that? We barely know one another."

"I know enough. We've become friends over the last year, and I've been holding back."

"Why, because you thought I was frail?" She scowls.

"Frail and Jane don't belong in the same sentence." I chuckle. "You are a remarkably tough, headstrong, independent woman. Did I mention beautiful too?" My gaze stays glued to hers. "What about me?"

Her brows draw together. "What about you?"

"I know you like me."

"I've found out tonight other women in this town like you too."

"I don't care about other women, Jane. Tell me."

"Are you fishing for a compliment?" She tries to leave my arms, but I hold her tighter.

"Only from you."

"Well...you're fiercely protective."

"And?" I cock an eye at her.

"Smart."

"What else, Jane?"

"You want a list?" She swallows hard.

"If you have one, then yes." I laugh.

"Fine. You're handsome and sexy. That's a rare combination to find in a man." Her gaze moves side to side, trying to avoid eye contact with me.

I still her with a finger raising her chin, forcing

her to look at me. When she does, I softly kiss her lips. They part ever so slightly, and I deepen the kiss. She pulls back, licking her lips. "I'm only a first base kinda girl on a first date."

"I'm okay with that." I kiss her again. This time, her hand grasps my shirt, dragging me closer to her. I can't keep my body from reacting.

Her giggle tickles my lips, vibrating against them. "I think part of you is not okay with it."

"Ignore it," I rasp.

"Um, it's *hard* to ignore."

"Trust me, you ain't telling me anything I don't already know." I kiss her again until she's breathless, her chest heaving for either air or from the passion I ignited within her.

"Maybe second base would be okay."

"You've got me so worked up I've forgotten how far second base is." I walk her backward until she's pressed against the wall. She grabs the hem of my shirt, pushing upward over my chest and shoulders. I lean down, allowing her to pull it over my head. Her gaze roams my body, stopping on a scar on my right lower side that runs down my side, tucked under my belt.

"What's this from?" she asks as she squats, laying her fingertip on the raised edge.

"My appendix ruptured when I was ten."

Her soft lips land on it as her hands unbuckle my belt, then slowly unzips my jeans. "I want to see it," she says softly.

I push my jeans down below my hips. She kisses every inch of it, making me hard as hell. "Do you have any more?" she asks.

"Scars?" I watch her eyes blink.

She nods.

I lower my jeans to my knees. "This one." I point to one that runs from the top of my left thigh to the inside of my knee. "This one is from a dirt bike accident when I was sixteen," I rasp.

Her finger traces the line of the scar. She stares up at me for a moment before she's removing my boxers. One of her small hands cups me as the other one lightly strokes me.

"Jane," I moan her name.

She hesitates for a second, then I disappear between her sweet lips. Bracing one hand on the wall, I glory in the feeling of her warm mouth. Her teeth softly dig into my skin as she sucks, then draws back up to the tip.

"Damn," I grit out. My entire body tenses, but my hips rock into her. "I love what you are doing, but you have to stop." I drag her up by her shoulders. "This is not how I want this to go down between us." Placing my hand behind her neck, I kiss her, pressing her body against the wall again. I unfasten her skinny jeans, and she wiggles out of them along with her panties. Grasping her thigh, I lift her leg over my hip, with my cock between us.

Her gaze goes downward. "I want you inside of me."

"I'm pretty sure that's beyond second base," I say, wanting it to be her choice.

She splays her hands on my chest, forcing me to inch backward. She arches and guides me inside her. It's heaven and hell at the same time.

"Jane," I say her name again, my jaw flexing. Her gaze locks with mine.

Gently kissing the sensitive skin of her neck, I take one hand and unbutton her white blouse. I feel her body tense instantly. She shoves me back and pushes me out of her. "I'm sorry. I can't do this. I thought I could, but I can't." She's frantically trying to put her jeans on.

I pull my boxers and jeans over my hips. "What's wrong? Did I hurt you?"

"No." I see her swipe a tear.

"Who did?"

"Nobody." She hesitates. "It's just that I'm not perfect like you." She's fully clothed.

It dawns on me the way she took in my scars. I'd forgotten about her kidney transplant. I can't believe this beautiful, intelligent woman is self-conscious to the point where she's afraid of me seeing her.

I inch closer to her, and her eyes widen. I trail my finger over the collar of her blouse, pushing the silky material to where the top of her lacy bra is showing. I lean down, kissing the swell of her breast. "I don't give a damn about your scars. All I want is your heart."

"Please take me home," she gasps slightly.

I stand tall with my hands on the wall behind her. "You're beautiful, Jane. I'll tell you every day until you believe it. I'll walk around naked with all my scars showing to prove to you that none of that matters to me."

"It matters to me," she sniffs.

"It shouldn't, and I'll rip apart the bastard who made you feel otherwise."

"I just want to go home. Please."

"Then I'll take you." I throw my shirt over my head, take her hand, and lead her to my truck. Opening her door, she climbs inside. "I would never hurt you, Jane," I say.

"I know you wouldn't," she responds.

She doesn't speak on the drive to the mill. I shove the truck in park and move to get out. Her words stop me.

"You don't have to walk me inside." She opens the

door, hopping out. She holds her arms snuggly against her body. "I'm sorry for the way tonight turned out. I tried to tell you it wouldn't work between us."

"You're the only one holding back. I've made my feelings known, and I don't plan on giving up so easily."

She shuts the door, and I watch her stroll into the Magnolia. When I glance out the back window, I see her painting. Stretching over the seat, I pick it up.

"I have the perfect spot for you in my room," I say to myself. "She doesn't know it yet, but she belongs there too."

CHAPTER EIGHT
JANE

"Jane, the interview for the livestock position will be happening in fifteen minutes." My assistant pokes her head in my office door.

"Tell the councilmen they can proceed without me," I respond, not looking up from my computer. I can't face Ethan after last night.

"Unfortunately, according to our city bylaws, the mayor has to actively participate in the hiring of this position."

"If they want to hire him, I'll sign the paperwork."

Paisley sits in the chair in front of my desk. "They won't hire him unless you are in on the interview."

I glance over my computer. "Go away, Paisley."

She stands, walking out of the office. "I'll tell them you'll be five minutes late," she says over her shoulder.

"Damn it." I dial Molly's number at work.

"MC Investments."

I love that she changed the name of her company when she married my brother. "Hey, Molls, it's Jane."

"Thanks for girls' night out. It was so much fun." I can hear her smile through the phone.

"Not much of girls' night when I end up all alone because the Calhoun women are one horny bunch."

"I'll plan the next one," she snickers.

I glance at my watch. "I only have about five minutes, and I need to talk to someone."

"What's up? You sound so serious."

"The interview with Ethan is happening in my boardroom in a few minutes."

"So."

I cover the receiver with my hand. "I ended up at his place last night."

"It's about damn time!" she hoots.

"Nothing happened...well, a little happened, but I can't face him today."

"Did you have sex or not?"

"I'm not sure how to answer your question."

"Girl, if you don't know if you screwed him or not, it's been far too long for you." She laughs.

"What am I going to do? I can't see him." I rest back in my chair.

"You're going to pull up your big girl panties and

do your job. Whatever happened between the two of you should not affect his career."

"You're right. Thanks, Molly."

"Don't think that you've gotten away without telling me details. I want to know what happened between the two of you."

"I gotta go. Love you, Molls." I hang up quickly.

Opening my desk drawer, where I keep my purse, I take out a light shade of pink lipstick and apply it. Standing, I straighten my knee-length gray pin-striped skirt and tuck in my pink satin top. Flipping open my compact, I take a look in the small mirror at my reflection. I tuck blond strands of hair behind my ears, slip my heels on and march like the professional I am to my office door.

"You can do this, Jane." I give myself a pep talk. Walking directly to the boardroom, through the large window I see Ethan, and Boone's back to me. The other men have already taken a seat around the oval table.

Putting on my business face, I step into the room. "Gentleman," I say, only keeping my gaze on Ethan for a millisecond.

"Mayor Calhoun," Ethan says coolly, holding his hand in my direction.

All eyes are on me. Gathering strength, I shake his hand. His touch instantly makes me feel warm.

"Mr. York," I say. "Have a seat, gentleman, so we can get this process underway.

The men immediately start asking Ethan questions. He doesn't miss a beat, tossing out numbers. He rattles them off as if he doesn't have to think about them. I realize how smart of a man Ethan really is. And, sexy. Don't go there, Jane, I tell myself. He looks good in a sports coat over his white button-down and dark blue jeans. They hug his ass nicely. A flash of me on my knees in front of him last night fills my mind. He's got the most beautiful cock I've ever seen. Not that I've seen a lot, but damn. His ripped body from hard manual labor makes my mouth drool. I involuntarily wipe my chin.

"You okay, Jane?" Boone's deep voice brings me back to the boardroom.

"Yes, I'm fine."

Out of my periphery, I see Ethan grin.

Bastard. He knows exactly what I was daydreaming about. "Have you gentlemen asked Mr. York all of your questions?"

"I think Boone is correct. Mr. York will be perfect for the job under Boone's guidance. I say we make the offer."

The other councilmen agree.

"Maybe he'd like some time to think it over," I say, turning in his direction.

"Thank you, but I'd like to accept it. I've been looking for a new challenge, and this one is right up my alley."

"You do know you have to work directly under Mayor Calhoun for the first ninety days," Bob adds.

"I'm aware." Ethan doesn't crack a smile.

"Good, then it's official. Ethan York is the new livestock agent for the town of Salt Lick." Bob stands, shaking his hand to congratulate him. The other men follow suit. "We'll celebrate your new position at the Cattleman's Restaurant tomorrow night at seven," he says.

"If you'll excuse me, I have other business to attend to." I rise. "I'm sure you will be the right man for the job," I say to Ethan with a smile. "I'll have my assistant get you all the paperwork, including the salary for the position. I move around the table and make my way back to my office. A few minutes later, Ethan is leaning in my doorway with his Stetson in his hand.

"May I come in?" he asks.

I nod.

He enters, shutting the door behind him.

"I'm sorry about last night," I start. "You and I have to come to some agreement to keep this professional."

He lays his hat on my desk, walking around to my

side and turns my chair facing him. "In this office, we can keep it as professional as you want." His voice is sexy. I swallow hard. "Outside this office, things are just heating up. I told you last night, I want your heart, and I have every intention of getting what I want."

"I..."

"I'm not done."

He kneels. "You're a beautiful, sexy woman. Your scars mean nothing to me. I take that back. They mean you're alive. You would've been dead if it wasn't for the surgery, and that makes them even more beautiful to me. You can hide it, but I promise I will kiss every inch of your scars, whether they be inside or out, and I'll heal your thoughts of hiding from me."

My hand trembles as I reach out to touch his face. "Why do you have to be so darn sweet?"

"I'm not. I'm being truthful. I've sat on the sidelines with you far too long. You already own my heart."

"What if I get sick and you change your mind? There's always the possibility of my body rejecting the kidney."

"I won't change my mind. I'll take care of you if that's the case."

"I can't ask you to do that."

"You're not asking."

"I'm scared."

He pulls a small box out of his pocket. "I'm not. I know what I want, and it's you." He opens it up, and it's a silver ring with a large square diamond in the middle. "Marry me, Jane."

My mouth nearly hits the floor. "You want to marry me?"

"It's the only way to show you how serious I am about you. I've loved you from a distance but no more."

"I don't want to hurt you, Ethan, but I'm not ready for marriage, and I don't know that I ever will be."

A sting fills his dark eyes. "Then I'll take what you can give me, and I'll wait for more."

"But what if there isn't any more?"

He stands. "You have so much love to give, Jane. I see it in your eyes."

I fight back my tears, wanting to rush into his arms, then I recall I can never give him the one thing he wants. "I can't, Ethan." My lip stiffens, knowing I'm hurting him.

He stuffs the box back into his pocket, picks up his Stetson, and places it on his head. "I'm not giving up," he says, then opens the door, walking out.

I pound my forehead on the desk. "I'm such an idiot. Ethan is the best man I could ever ask for." I raise my head with tears streaming down. But I'm not the best woman for him. He deserves a woman who can give him a family. My health could take a turn at any moment. My hand arbitrarily rubs the length of my scar. I rush to the bathroom, locking the door behind me. Lifting my blouse, the raised, angry scar looks hideous. It starts below my ribcage and runs in a crescent moon pattern down to my pubic bone. It's a constant reminder to me that my health could change at any moment and that I will never bear children. I have to build my life knowing that. Staying focused on my career to the point I don't have time to think about what I'm missing out on. Ethan will find someone else. In fact, I could introduce him to several women I've seen salivating over him.

I wash the tears from my face. "That's it. I'll solve this problem by having him fall in love with someone else," I sniff.

Rushing back to my office, I snatch my purse and keys so I can go help Margret at the Magnolia. She puts the kiddos down this time of day for a nap, and I cover the needs of the bed and breakfast.

Plowing through town, I hear sirens behind me. "Damn it, Mike. Why do you always have to stop me?" Turning the wheel, I park on the side of the road. I tap the steering wheel, waiting for him to be in my window.

"License and registration." He holds out his hand.

"It hasn't changed since the last time you stopped me," I snark.

"This time, I'm writing you a ticket." He leans his elbows on the open window.

I yank open the glove box. "You can write it, but I ain't paying it."

"Why do all you Calhoun women have to be such a pain in my arse?" He grins.

"It's in our genes." I smirk in response.

"Please don't fly through town anymore. It looks bad when our own mayor can't obey the law."

"I ain't making any promises. Are we done here?" I wave the papers at him.

He stands, tucking his thumbs under his belt. "For today, but I'm sure knowing you, we'll be right back here tomorrow."

I slam the glove box shut after putting the registration back inside. "Have a good day, Officer Mike. I'll have to let the mayor know you're doing a fantastic job." I peel out, heaving dust in the air.

I don't stop until I'm parked at the bed and breakfast. "Sorry I'm late," I say, running inside. "Mike pulled me over again." I place my purse under the counter.

"It's alright. The twins just finished eating." Margret has both heavy-eyed toddlers in her lap. She wheels toward the back of the house. "Oh, before I forget," she stops, turning toward me. "There is a gentleman who checked into room 203 says he knows you."

"Where's he from?" I scowl. Everyone I know lives in Salt Lick.

"Texas." She rolls down the hall into one of the back rooms.

"Texas? Maybe he's an old classmate." I flip through the registration book until I see a familiar name. "Matthew Billings," I gasp. "What the hell is he doing here?" I want nothing to do with him, and if Noah sees him, he's likely to kill him.

"There you are. I've been looking all over this godforsaken town for you. I heard you're the mayor." Matthew comes up beside me. "It's good to see you, Jane."

"The feeling is not mutual. What the hell do you want?" I grasp the edge of the counter so my fist doesn't make contact with his nose.

"That's no way to greet your fiancé."

"I recall you ended things between us a long time ago."

His gaze roams my body. "Rumor is you're just fine. You got your transplant and are healthy as a horse."

"It's none of your business how I am."

He tries to tuck a piece of hair behind my ear, but I dart out of his reach. "Don't be like that. You and I were good together before you got sick. I've come here to make amends."

"The only thing you need to do is leave," I seethe, pointing toward the door.

"Look, I know I was an ass. I've grown up since then, and I'm aware how I treated you was wrong. I love you, Jane."

"You wouldn't know what love was if it bit you in the ass!" I yell.

"Is there a problem here?" Wyatt comes through the front door, storming to the rescue.

"I'd like this man to gather his things and leave the property."

"I've already paid for a month in advance." He squares off with Wyatt.

"If the lady wants you to leave, I'll refund your money." Wyatt doesn't bow down to him.

I touch his arm. "It's okay. He can stay. Our season is winding down, and I don't know if we can fill the vacancy."

"I don't care about the money," Wyatt says, protectively.

"It doesn't affect me one way or another if he's here or not. Just stay out of my way." I stand beside Wyatt.

"How am I supposed to win you back if I can't be near you?"

Wyatt's brows draw together when he stares at me.

"Long story," I say, "from a lifetime ago."

CHAPTER NINE
CHET

"Girls, I'm afraid Scarlet needs to go for a walk," Winnie says as she dusts the flour from her hands. She and the girls have been baking cookies for hours.

"Grandpa can let her out," Missy says, licking cookie dough from her fingers.

"I couldn't ask him to do that." Winnie unties her apron.

"Please, Grandpa," Rose begs.

I hold my hand out in front of me. "Fine, I'll take the rat out."

"She'll need a sweater on. The evenings here are a bit chilly." Winnie fixes her apron.

"I'm not putting no damn sweater on a dog," I grumble.

"You really shouldn't swear in front of the children," Winnie scolds.

"Trust me, they've heard much worse." I chuckle.

"At least put her on a leash." Winnie points to a pink leash with jewels running the length of it.

I appease her, grabbing it. "Come on, Scar." I open the door. Her head tilts up at me, then she looks at Winnie.

"She prefers to be carried and placed in the grass." Winnie smiles.

"What she prefers and what's she's gonna get is a boot scooting her out the door."

"Grandpa!" Missy yells.

"I'm only kidding." I begrudgingly pick up the furless princess. I unsnap her leash as soon as I'm outside. "Dogs don't belong on a leash," I mutter.

The sky is filled with different shades of orange as the sun is starting its descent from the long day. Walking out into a grassy area near the barn, I put the pampered pup in the grass, hoping she'll do her business quickly. She prances around as if she doesn't like the evening dew that's settled on the ground.

"You are one ugly four-legged critter." The thing stares up at me as if she knows what I said. "Don't look at me like that. I'm not the one who has no fur and appears to have a goatee on the top of my head."

She struts around a few times in a circle before she squats to pee.

I hear a growl coming from the distance. "Shit." I see the gray eyes of a coyote prowling closer. I always grab my shotgun to carry with me this time of the evening; instead, I carried Scar.

"Get on out of here!" I yell, waving my arms, but the creature creeps closer. Moving slowly, I lean down, picking up the dog, tucking her under my arm.

"She ain't your dinner, and neither am I." The coyote is skinny and looks as if he's starving. He's unlikely to give up easily. When he starts to move faster, I take off in a run, trying to make it into the barn before he can get to me. I misstep, rolling my ankle in a hole. My hat flies off, and I'm able to push Scar out of the way before I crush her under my weight. When I do, my body slams into a pile of freshly cut wood Bear stacked on the side of the barn. Scar has her body pressed against the wall, and she's shaking like a leaf. I roll to face the predator still stalking us. Pain sears through my ankle as I try to get up. Dragging my body closer to Scar, I'm able to reach a piece of the wood. The coyote is within inches of me when I turn, swinging as hard as I can. It knocks him to the ground, but he regains his footing quickly, snarling at me.

"Get the hell out of here!" I holler, waving the

wood in his direction. It doesn't scare him one bit. He lunges at me. His teeth grind into the wood as I hold him back. Scar starts barking and nipping at his front paw. She distracts him enough for me to grasp another piece of wood and slam it into his ribcage. He falters and runs a few feet back.

I pick up Scar and get up, using the wall for support, and I'm able to make it inside the barn, closing the door before the scrawny beast regains its strength. I slam the door shut and hear the thing hit it with its body. Its claws scrape down the door like nails on a chalkboard.

"You're safe, girl." I hold the dog out to examine her. "Winnie might kill me if something happened to you."

Hobbling over to the shelf where Boone charges the radios, I grab one. "Boone, you copy?"

The radio buzzes with static before he answers. "Copy."

"I'm held up in the barn with a hungry coyote outside. I left my shotgun on the porch. Winnie and the kiddos are in the house. I'm afraid if I'm gone too long, they might come looking for me."

"I'm on my way." The radio clicks off.

It ain't long before I hear a shot, and the barn door swings open. "You still in here?" Boone marches in with the shotgun still gripped in his hand.

"Yeah. Did you get him?" I put Scar on the ground when I see Winnie and the girls headed our way.

"You okay, Grandpa?" Missy asks, stopping next to Boone.

Scar jumps into Winnie's arms.

"I think my ankle is broken. Won't know until we get my boot off." I limp toward Boone, and he hustles over to me, placing my arm over his shoulder to help me back to the main house. He helps me in the recliner and starts removing my boot.

"You saved Scarlet." Winnie has tears in her eyes.

"She saved me, too, so I guess we're even." She places her on the floor, and the damn critter jumps in my lap.

I grip the arm of the chair as Boone eases my foot out of the boot, then my sock. "He's going to need ice," Boone says, inspecting my ankle.

"I'll get it." Winnie rushes out of the living room.

"You're gonna have to go to the hospital for X-rays." Boone gently places my foot on the floor.

"Nonsense. It will be fine."

Boone gets up, taking his cell phone from his back pocket. "I'm calling Clem to come look at it."

Winnie comes back with a large baggie of ice and a towel. Bending over, she pushes the recliner back to lift my feet. Then she positions the towel on my ankle before she gently puts the ice on top of it.

"It looks awful swollen already," she says. Scar looks back and forth between us, then curls up on my shoulder. "I think you've made a friend for life." She strokes her furless body.

"For a rat, she ain't so bad." I chuckle. Winnie's blue eyes sparkle. Having her here makes me miss Amelia. I place my rough hand on her delicate one. "I'll be fine. Don't you worry."

"Would it be alright if I get a few of my things and stay here to help you until your ankle heals?"

This house is lonely at spells. It'd be nice having her here, and it might be weeks before I'm back on my feet. "I'd like that."

As soon as Clem rushes in the door, Boone takes Winnie to her place.

"Daddy, Boone's right. You need to have this looked at. Even if it ain't broken, it's a bad sprain, and you're going to need a walking boot." She's taken off the layer of ice and towel to examine it. "You're lucky the coyote didn't win. Why didn't you have your shotgun?"

"I was distracted unhooking Scar from her leash."

Clem rubs the dog's skin. "I think she likes you."

"The feeling ain't mutual."

Clem snickers. "Right." She stands. "I'm glad the

two of you are okay, but I still think we need to take you to the emergency room. I'll run the girls to Bear's house, and Boone and I can take you."

"Fine."

She leads the girls out, and Boone returns with Winnie. "Clem says you agreed to go to the hospital."

"I did."

"I'll get the kitchen cleaned up while you're gone," Winnie adds. I smile, thinking about her cleaning. She's indicated many times she had maids for that sorta thing. I was surprised she knew how to bake cookies.

"You just make sure to save me some of those cookies that have been smelling up the house."

She tucks her hair behind her ear, and I think how purdy she is. It's been a long time since I was attracted to anyone but Amelia. The two women couldn't be more opposite.

"Let's get this nonsense over with." I put the foot of the recliner down, and Boone helps me up.

CHAPTER TEN

JANE

I've been in town most of the day and been able to avoid a run-in with Matthew. I was so thankful he was nowhere around when I made it to the Magnolia. Of course, coming in the back entry helped a lot. I don't have time to deal with him, nor do I want to. I want to get a shower and curl my hair before meeting Ethan and the councilmen for dinner at the Cattleman's.

I quickly strip out of my work clothes and wash my hair under the spray of the hot shower. Drying off, I cover my hair in a towel and slip on a robe. I then brush my hair, blow it out, and curl it into waves of blond.

I open the drawer to pull out my basket of makeup, and someone knocks on the door. "Please, don't be Matthew." I pad quietly across the floor, peer through the peephole and see Ethan.

Opening the door, my mouth waters. He's wearing dark blue dress jeans, a white button-down, and a tweed sports jacket. The word yummy comes to mind. "What are you doing here? I thought we were meeting at the restaurant." I open the door wide for him to come inside my tiny room.

He tosses his black Stetson on my bed. "I thought it'd be nice to go together."

"As you can see"—I glance down at my robe —"I'm far from ready."

"I can wait," he says, sitting on the small couch.

"Suit yourself." I shrug and return to the mirror in my bathroom, leaving the door open so I can see him. "Are you excited about your new position?" I ask as I apply my makeup.

"I'm looking forward to it, among other things." I hear him making a noise but don't look as I apply my mascara. I make sure to smear it on thick. I lean back to check it out, and Ethan is standing in the bathroom door stark naked.

I blink, making sure I'm not imagining it, then turn toward him. "What are you doing?"

"Getting comfortable."

"Um, we're supposed to be going out to dinner. I

don't think your current attire is acceptable." I slowly gaze over his gorgeous body.

"When you're done gettin' dressed, I'll put my clothes back on," he says, nonchalantly.

"Does this have something to do with the other night?" I bite my bottom lip.

He steps up next to me. "My scars don't bother me. Yours shouldn't stop you from loving who you are."

"And you think you being naked will make me less self-conscious with my own scars?"

"That's the plan." He walks buck naked to my bed and plops down.

I follow him. "So, every time you're around me, you plan on being naked?" I point my mascara container at him.

He sits. "When we're not in public."

"You're being ridiculous." I roll my eyes at him and walk over to my closet. Does he think I mind him being naked? A hot man with muscles ripped over his body. Not to mention his beautiful junk. Two can play his game. I move several hangers of clothes out of the way. I'd planned on wearing a business suit, but I have the perfect dress for the evening. It's a deep emerald silky green that fits snuggly over my curves. It has spaghetti straps and dips low in the back, resting against my ass. I purchased it after my surgery, wanting to feel sexy again but never had an occasion to wear it.

Grabbing my undergarments, I sashay back into the bathroom, shutting the door behind me. Once I have my backless cami and panties on, I open the door, walking to my dresser as if I'm missing something. I can feel his eyes scorching every inch of my skin.

"Sorry. I forgot my stockings." I take them out along with a garter belt and bend over, slowly pulling them up my thighs.

I smile when I hear his groan. Turning to look at him, he's rolled to his side, propped up on this elbow and my bed pillow covering his midsection. He's no doubt sporting a hard-on.

Making sure my cami is covering my abdomen, I turn, walk toward him and bend over to pick up my high-heeled shoes, giving him a good look at my cleavage. "You hiding something, cowboy? I thought you were comfortable being naked." I grin.

"I was until you started dressing. I can't help how my body reacts to you." He sits on the edge of the bed, grasping my hips, drawing me close to him. "You're beautiful," he says, planting a kiss on the soft material of my cami, covering my belly button.

It sends a tingling warmth over my body. His fingers toy with the hem, but I jerk away. "We've got a dinner celebration to go to." I take the dress from its hanger and draw it over my head. "You should really get dressed now."

He stands, dropping the pillow to the floor. I swallow hard. I'd love nothing more than to push him back down on the bed and have an all-nighter with him.

He tugs on his jeans, tucking his hard cock inside. I hold back a lustful moan. Why oh why does he have to be so gorgeous? I've never seen a more perfect man. I've only been with Matthew, and I know for a fact he's got nothing on Ethan. Matt was okay in bed, but he wasn't very adventurous like I wanted him to be. In fact, we weren't very compatible at all. I wanted kink, and he was appalled by it. Looking back, I'm glad he broke things off with me. I would've never been happy with him.

"Are you ready?" he asks, placing his hat on his head.

I grab my cell phone, stashing it in my purse. "Yes."

He holds the door open for me, then sticks his elbow out for me to take. I'd forgotten all about Matt being here until I hear him asking Margret where I might be.

I try to rush Ethan out the door before he sees me but no such luck.

"I've been waiting for you to come home all day," he says, acting as if I'm not on Ethan's arm.

"Who are you?" Ethan's voice deepens.

"I'm her fiancé." Matt's shoulders seem to puff out.

"Ex," I add. "This is Matthew Billings."

"The idiot that dumped you after he found out you were sick." Ethan stares at him.

"I've apologized for being an 'idiot' as you say. I've come to take her back to Texas with me."

"You must be blind too," Ethan snickers.

"What?"

"Not only have you missed the fact that she's on my arm, but her entire body language also tells me she wants nothing to do with you. So, unless you'd like my fist to connect with your jaw, I suggest you leave the lady alone."

His fierce protectiveness of me makes my lady parts ache. I want to run up the stairs back to my room, yank off his clothes and not emerge for a couple of days.

Matt has the balls to step closer to me. "I think the lady can speak for herself."

Ethan's jaw twitches a few times. I hold tighter to his arm. "The lady has spoken. I told you earlier to go back to where you came from and leave me alone."

"You heard her," Ethan says, sternly.

Matt moves back. "I'm not going anywhere until I win her over. You two have a nice evening. She'll come to her senses sooner or later."

Ethan's body tenses. "He isn't worth it," I say as I turn us away from him and start walking.

"You knew he was in town," Ethan states, holding open his truck door.

"He checked into the bed and breakfast yesterday." He shuts the door and gets in his side, starting the engine. "I don't like him."

"He'll grow tired of me blowing him off and leave."

"He isn't your type."

"Yeah, well, I was young and blind. He was the first guy that really paid any attention to me."

"Did you love him?"

"I thought at the time I did. He broke my heart when he ended things between us. He made me feel like no man would ever want me again."

He takes his gaze off the road and stares at me. "He's a fucking coward." He looks back at the road. "I want you so badly it guts me."

My breath hitches in my throat at his admission. "Ethan." I say his name softly.

We don't speak another word between us on the way to the restaurant. He parks, hops out and opens my door. We stand staring at each other for a long moment.

I finally break the silence. "Let's go celebrate your new job." Taking his arm, we walk inside the only upscale restaurant in Salt Lick. Its décor matches its name. The seats are covered in red velvet. Large, framed pictures of cowboys are displayed on the dark walls. The councilmen are already seated at the table with glasses of whiskey in front of them. They stand, and Ethan pulls out a chair for me.

"What would you like to drink?" he asks.

"I'll take a glass of soda water with a lime." I scoot my chair under the table, and Ethan heads to the bar.

Bob moves his chair closer to mine. "You look very purdy tonight."

"Thank you." I watch Ethan at the bar when a redhead comes over to him. He obviously knows her when she greets him with a kiss to the cheek. A bite of jealously scorches my insides.

As she talks to him, he glances in my direction, catching me spying on him. He grins, then rubs his hand down her bare arm. I'm so focused on his every move, I don't feel Bob's arm on the back of my chair.

"Would you like me to order for you," he asks, smoothly.

"I'm more than capable of ordering for myself." I take a sip of ice water the waitress set in front of me.

Ethan picks up our drinks, and the woman toys with Ethan's shirt collar. He tells her goodbye and marches back over to our table. He places the glass by my napkin and sets his down before he sits.

Bob's hand rests in the middle of my back as he starts talking to the other men at the table. I squirm under his touch.

"I don't think the lady likes you touching her." Ethan glares at Bob's hand as if he could set it on fire.

He snatches it away. "Forgive me," he says. "I didn't realize the lady was spoken for."

"I'm not," I respond, "but that doesn't give you the right to touch me. I've asked you in the past to stop."

He raises his hands in surrender. "It won't happen again."

"Good," Ethan says.

The waitress comes around to take our orders. She starts with me and moves around the table. I lean over to Ethan. "Who was the woman at the bar?"

"What's it matter? You've made it clear we aren't a couple." I see the hurt in his eyes.

Dinner is served, and we celebrate Ethan's new job. The men at the table lay out their plans for his position, each telling him what they think the position takes to make it work for the town. Ethan is respectfully taking it all in. He's an intelligent man.

He'll make the job his own and impress the hell out of all of them.

The more I watch him interact with these men, the more I like him. He exudes confidence, not arrogance. Something I find incredibly attractive about a man. I'm extremely moved by his intelligence and ability to handle people. He's so much more than I ever knew, and the more I get to know him, the more I find myself wanting him.

The evening finally ends, and we head back to Magnolia Mill. "I think you fully won them all over. You're going to be a fantastic livestock agent. Just the change Salt Lick needed," I say as we amble up the steps to the front entrance.

I walk in, but he doesn't. "Good night, Jane."

I don't want him to leave. "Do you want to come in for a nightcap?"

He closes the distance between us, and I can feel his breath on my skin. "Only if I can stay for breakfast."

"I...I..."

He steps back. "If you have to think about it, then the answer is no." He kisses me sweetly before he backs out the door. "I'll see you at work tomorrow." He tilts his hat.

"You know, the ladies fall all over him." I hear

Wyatt's voice behind me. "If you want him, you shouldn't wait too long."

I move over to the counter, leaning on it. "I don't know what I want."

"It can't be that idiot upstairs." He points to the ceiling.

"Definitely not."

"What's your hold up? Ethan's a good guy."

"You wouldn't understand." I sigh.

"Try me."

I lay my purse on the counter and start pacing the tiled floor. "Did you ever think you weren't worthy of another person?"

"Yes," he says, without hesitation.

"Or that you were too ugly?" I keep pacing, and he comes from behind the counter, halting me with his hand on my shoulder.

"Yes, to both, but I can tell you, neither one of those things are true of you. How could you possibly think so?"

I rub my temples.

"Let me guess, the asshole from Texas made you feel that way."

I nod.

"He's wrong, and don't give him the satisfaction of believing him. I've been in your shoes, but it was me telling myself I wasn't worthy."

"How did you let go of the notion?"

"Margret."

I step on my tiptoes, kissing his cheek. "Thanks, Wyatt."

"Don't get stuck in that notion, or you're going to let something really good slip through your fingers."

"I'll keep it in mind. Good night, brother."

"Sleep well, Jane."

CHAPTER ELEVEN
ETHAN

I curse under my breath as I storm to my truck. What the hell is wrong with me? I should've said yes to her nightcap. Abruptly spinning around to go back inside before she takes her invite back, I run into Matthew. He's as tall as I am, but he's leaner, with no muscle tone. He looks like a guy who's done nothing but work behind a desk. The only thing he's lifted is a pencil.

"You leaving?" I ask, stepping back from him.

"No. I waited until the two of you came back. I could've marched inside and followed her to her room, but I chose to stay out here and speak to you. I know Jane was a mess when she left Texas, and that was partly my fault."

"Partly," I repeat, gruffly.

"Her illness took me by surprise. She was young

and beautiful. I never expected her to be sick, much less the prospect of dying. My career was just taking off. I didn't have time to be in and out of hospitals."

"What I'm hearing is that your life was more important than hers." I want to spit on his shoes.

"At the time, I wasn't willing to give up what I had worked for to take care of a sick fiancée."

"Get the hell out of my face!" I shove him.

"All that has changed. She's perfect again. I know I can make things up to her for my poor behavior."

I stomp toward him and grab him with both my hands by the collar. "And what about her scars! You created the one's she's got on the inside, and you can't handle the one's on the outside, you little weasel!"

"I know I said some hurtful things to her, but I've changed. I love her," he says as I push him away.

"A man that loves a woman accepts her for who she is inside and out. It's a man's job to love her more when she's broken, not kick her like a stray dog."

"You're afraid she'll pick me over you!" he yells.

"Not in this lifetime." I chuckle.

"Yeah, then why's she in her room alone tonight?" He wipes his mouth with the back of his hand.

"It's called respect for one another."

"She doesn't want you in her bed. The one thing I recall about Jane is that she had an appetite for sex. She always wanted more than I gave her."

I take off toward him, pinning him against one of the vehicles. "I'll fucking kill you if you talk about her that way again," I seethe as my glare bores into him. "You obviously have no idea what it means to please a woman, or she wouldn't have needed more." I draw him forward then toss him hard against the car. "Stay the hell away from her!"

Slamming my truck door and revving the engine, I'm tempted to run over his sorry ass. What the hell did she ever see in a guy like him? My headlights blind him as I haul ass out of the parking lot. I haven't been this angry in a long time. I hate the way he talks about Jane.

My phone rings, and I dig it out of my back pocket, answering it before I see who it is.

"Hello!"

"Hey, you okay?" Jane's voice is soft.

"Sorry. I'm fine." She calms me.

"I wanted to say I had a really good time tonight. I know it wasn't a date, but I enjoyed being on your arm."

"Me, too, but I want you to be comfortable in my arms."

"You're a little intimidating to me," she admits.

"Why? What can I do to make you more at ease?"

"Stop looking so damn good naked, for one." She giggles.

"My scars don't turn you off, so why do you think yours would make you any less desirable?"

She's so quiet for a moment, I think I've lost her.

"Jane?"

"I'm here."

"What's number two? You said for one."

"You...um..."

"What? I really want to know."

"You seem like you like control." Her words come out in a whisper.

I gather her meaning from the conversation I had with her ex-fiancé. I turn my truck around without slowing down, hitting the shoulder of the road and bouncing back in her direction.

"I aim to prove to you I can give up control to you." I hit End, tossing the phone on the seat. As I park at the Magnolia, there is no sign of Matt. My boots make a loud noise as I stomp up the wooden steps and swing open the door. Wyatt is behind the counter. I tilt my head at him, and he smiles.

"She's in her room," he says, grinning and tossing me a key card. "She'll thank me later."

I trod up to her floor and insert the key. She's standing in front of her window, wearing a long peach-colored nightgown and a silky robe.

"What the hell, Ethan?" She whirls in my direction.

I throw the key card on the nightstand, lay my hat on the lamp, and meet her at the window.

"Tell me what you want, Jane. Whatever it is, you can have it."

Her painted fingernail is at her lip. "Turn off the overhead light and switch on the lamp," she says.

I do as she asks and return to her.

"What now?"

She reaches for my belt, unbuckling it. I don't move, letting her have complete control. Once it's unfastened, she whips it out of its loops, throwing it on the floor.

"Take off your jacket and shirt." Her pupils are as dark as I've ever seen them.

I finagle my shoulders free of my jacket, tossing it on the back of the couch. Next, I unbutton my shirt.

She tucks her hands under my collar and removes my shirt. "Now your jeans." Her tone is soft and sexy.

I kick out of my boots, taking my jeans and boxers off. Inhaling, I stand tall.

Her gaze roams my body. She leisurely moves around me as her hand traces my hip, then my ass. I can hear her breathing faster as she admires me. My head falls back when her lips gently touch my shoulder. I have to force myself not to take control of the situation.

Reaching my hand behind me for hers, she takes

it, slowly inching in front of me. Her stare is scorching my body.

"Your turn," I say, tugging at the soft belt of her robe.

She takes a step back, and I think I've lost her again. As her hand trembles, she loosens the tie. My gaze locks with hers. Letting her robe fall to her feet, I can see the outline of her breasts through the thin material. Her nipples are perky and tight. Her chest heaves as I take her in from head to toe.

I wait quietly for her to continue as she hesitantly gnaws on her bottom lip.

She edges the satin material up her legs, gathering it in her hands. She stops at the top of her thighs, watching my reaction. When she sees nothing but love pouring out of me, she draws it up further.

She's bare and beautiful. Pulling it up an inch further, I can see the start of her scar. Agonizingly slowly, she inches the material over her belly, then her breasts, until she's completely naked in front of me.

Her scar runs in a crescent moon shape right above her pubic area to the lower part of her ribs on the right side. None of it takes away from how gorgeous she is.

I close the gap between us, reaching my hand to her skin. I get on my knees and kiss her scar as I stare into her eyes. "You are beautiful."

Her hand trembles again as she touches my hair. She closes her eyes, and I get up. "What do you want now, Jane?"

She points to the bed. "Sit."

I do without thinking about it.

She stands between my parted legs, placing her finger beneath my chin. "I'm afraid if I tell you what I want, you'll leave."

"I won't. I promise."

She gets down on her knees then bends over my lap. Looking over her shoulder at me, she says, "I want you to spank me."

I don't let her see that I'm shocked. I've never spanked a woman in my life. For whatever reason, she needs this from me.

Rubbing my hand on her backside as if I'm trying to prepare the spot where I'll smack her, she drops her head.

"I don't want to hurt you," I say.

"You won't."

Raising my hand, I slap her ass.

She arches slightly, letting out a moan. Not of pain but pleasure.

I do it again, a little harder this time. Her skin instantly turns pink with my handprint on her ass.

"Again," she rasps.

After spanking her one more time, she goes to her

knees as her mouth crashes against mine. I can feel how turned on she is with each swipe of her tongue.

"Thank you," she cries as her fingers pull my hair.

"What else do you want, Jane?" I ask, between brutal kisses.

"Just you," she answers.

I pick her up, laying her on the bed beside me and running my hands all over her body. She's so freaking turned on, I'm not sure I'll be able to control myself. Making my way down to her nipple, I draw it between my teeth. She moans, and I give it a little tug.

She gasps loudly, "yes." Her hands land on my shoulder, and she pushes me hard until I'm flat on my back. "I want to be in control," she hisses, then scrapes her nails down my chest as she climbs on top of me. Grasping my cock, she hovers over me and slides down with so much force I almost come inside her. Rocking her hips back and forth, inching me deeper, her head falls back in pleasure. Grabbing her hips, I sit and suck on her nipple. Her head pops back up, and her fingers dip into my shoulders as she raises and lowers herself onto me.

"You feel so damn tight," I grit between my teeth, staving off my orgasm. I reach between us and maneuver my fingers so I can touch her. She hisses again, and I move harder and faster.

"Ethan!" she roars seconds before her body wraps tighter around my cock. I hold on, enjoying the way her body has reacted until I can take no more. She kisses me as I let go.

Her head falls on my shoulder, and I wrap my arms around her waist. My face is nuzzled against her chest, and I can hear the pounding of her heart as she tries to catch her breath.

Rolling her off me, I tuck into her backside and softly kiss her neck. "You okay?" I whisper.

She nods.

"I didn't hurt you, did I?"

"No. Thank you for giving me what I needed."

"Do you want to talk about it?"

She rolls over to face me. "I've only ever had sex with one man."

"Matthew," I say.

She presses her fingertips to my lips.

"Sex was always the same. Missionary position, and I wasn't allowed to touch him. He never once asked me what I wanted."

"You wanted him to spank you?" I watch her eyes closely.

"No. I don't know what came over me, but I wanted it from you in that moment." She bites her lip. "Have you ever spanked a woman before?"

"No. I've never raised a hand to a woman."

"Did you hate it?" Her gaze rocks back and forth with mine.

"I only hated the thought of hurting you."

"It did quite the opposite." She blushes.

"I'm not used to a woman being in charge, Jane, but I'll give you whatever you need as long as you let me have some control too."

"I think I'd like that." She smiles.

I kiss her and spend the next several hours making love to her. I don't stop her any time she wants to touch me or change positions. It seemed to bring her great joy exploring my body and even greater happiness when I returned the favor. I fell asleep curled next to her, stroking her hair.

WHEN I WAKE UP, THE BED IS EMPTY. "JANE."

She pops out of the bathroom, fully dressed and brushing her hair. "You're late for your first day on the job."

I spin the clock on the nightstand in my direction. "Shit!" I say, jumping out of bed. "It's nine o'clock. Why didn't you wake me?" I tug on the boxers and jeans I wore last night.

"We were up so late I thought you needed the sleep. I can easily make an excuse for you."

I pull my button-down over my shoulders, leaving it open as I put on my boots. "I have to run by the house and change. I can't show up in the same clothes I wore to dinner."

"Don't rush. I'll tell them you were working on the computer, studying the market prices. That is part of your job," she says, smiling.

I pick up my jacket, place a quick kiss to her lips and open the door. "I'll see you at work."

She grabs my hand before I walk out. "I enjoyed last night, but can we keep this between the two of us at work?"

"Will do, boss lady," I say, putting my Stetson on.

"I'm not your boss," she hollers as I walk down the hallway to the stairs.

As I hit the bottom landing, Margret sees me and smiles from ear to ear. "I see you two finally worked things out," she says.

I glance down at my bare chest. Stopping at the counter, I lay my jacket down and button my shirt. "Don't say a word to her about it."

"Oh, you know I will." She laughs.

I give her a stern look, and she laughs harder. "Damn Calhoun women," I mutter, heading out the door.

CHAPTER TWELVE
BEAR

"What the hell happened to you?" Daddy is making his way to the barn as I do a circle on the four-wheeler headed to feed the cattle.

"I had a run-in with a coyote last night."

"Did it bite you?" I climb off.

"No. I fell in a hole and twisted my ankle, trying to save Scar from being his dinner."

"Where was your shotgun?"

"I made the unwise choice of choosing a pampered pet's leash over it."

"What are you doing walking that thang? I thought you didn't like it." I stare down at his walking boot.

"She's kinda growing on me." He yanks off his hat, wiping his brow with his sleeve.

"The dog or Ethan's mom?" I chuckle.

"Did you need something, boy, because I believe you have work that needs to be done," he grumbles.

I grip his shoulder. "Why would I want to work when it's more fun razzing you? Besides, I think it would be good for you to get back in the saddle, so to speak."

"You'd be wise to mind your own business, boy." He points his crooked finger at my chest, and his usual scowl deepens.

I laugh. "You quit scaring me a long time ago. I know underneath all that hot air your blowing, you'd never harm one of your own children."

He grabs the pitchfork leaning against the barn. "Don't bet on it."

I take a step back. "Alright, truce, old man."

Missy and Rose are headed our way, holding boxes they use to collect the eggs.

"Hey, Daddy," Missy says, shielding her eyes from the morning sun.

"Why aren't you two in school today?"

"It's a teacher's workday," Rose chimes in. "Momma and Aunt Nita sent us out to the chicken pen. We're going into town to trade them for chicken feed."

"When we're done, Grandma York said our dresses and hats for the Derby this weekend arrived at her house this morning, so we're going to go try them on." Missy is all too cheerful for this time of day.

"Grandma York?" I raise a brow.

"That's what she said we could call her." Missy shrugs one shoulder.

"Don't forget your momma is picking you up tomorrow to spend a few days with her," I tell Missy.

Her face twists into a scowl.

"What's wrong?" I pull her pigtail.

"Nothing."

"Did something happen last time you were there?"

"No, Daddy."

"I've been looking all over for the two of you," Ethan's mom says, walking in our direction. "Clem called and said you were coming to the main house after collecting the eggs."

"We got a little sidetracked," Rose says, opening her hand that's full of blackberries.

Winifred picks one up out of her hand, popping it in her mouth. "These are delicious. I bet your grandma has a recipe for pie somewhere in the kitchen."

Ethan moseys up beside her. "Since when do you cook? First the cookies and now pie? My entire life, I don't recall you being in the kitchen."

"Don't you look handsome." She kisses his cheek.

"Didn't you start your new job today?" I ask.

"Yeah, I'm running late. I need to go to the cottage and change clothes."

"Those digs are too fancy for your line of work." Daddy points at him.

"Right, that's why I'm changing."

"I think he looks fine." His mom pinches his cheek as if he were a five-year-old.

"Don't you be thinking you becoming the live-stock agent gets you out of your chores around here, son," my old man grumbles.

"You can't expect him to work all day and then come home to work some more." Winifred squares off with him.

"I most certainly can. He's living on my property, and he'll earn his keep like anyone else around here."

"It's okay, Mom. I don't mind." Ethan tries to cool her off.

"I'm living here now, so I'll earn my keep and his. Tell me how much you want, and I'll write you a check."

"I don't want your money." He waves her off.

"Then you'll put me to work around here like anyone else," she huffs.

"Mom," Ethan tries to interject.

"I may have lived a pampered life, as you so

frequently point out, but never let it be said that a York doesn't pay their way." She folds her arms over her chest.

"Now, Winnie, don't go get your feathers all ruffled. There is no way I'm having you muck the barn."

She rolls up her expensive sleeves. "I'm more than capable of pulling my own weight." She jerks the pitchfork from his hands.

Then Ethan reaches over, snatching it free of her hands. "I'll take care of the barn before I change. Why don't you take the girls inside and find the recipe for the pie?"

She turns her head, sticking her nose in the air. "I'll do just that." She looks at the girls. "As soon as you're done collecting the eggs, we'll go to my house, then we'll find the spot you picked those blackberries." She struts off.

"I see you haven't lost your charm." I laugh, gripping the old man's shoulder.

"I'll never understand women," he mutters. He limps to the barn. "You can't live with them and... nope, that's it, you can't live with them," he says before he disappears.

I turn toward Ethan. "Those clothes you're sportin' speak loudly of the walk of shame."

"I've got work to get done," he says, storming off.

"I'm just saying I'm happy if you and Jane finally hooked up," I holler. I climb back on the four-wheeler and head for the hay bales to feed the cattle. I don't hear my phone ringing until I park.

"What do you want, Sandy?"

"Good morning to you too, Bradley."

I hate when she calls me by my given name. It only sounds good coming from Nita's lips. "I've got work to do and no time for chitchat."

"I want to change my time with Missy this week."

"Why, what happened?"

"Nothing. I'm going out with some friends from work tonight, so I wanted to wait to get her on Friday."

"The Derby is this weekend, and you know it."

"Right. She invited me to go with her."

"Not happening. It's a family affair."

"I'm her mother." Her voice fills with anger.

"Nita and I want to enjoy the time with her. It's not your weekend, and it ain't my fault you're ditching her for your girlfriends. You drinking again?"

"No. We're just hanging out to celebrate birthdays this month. I haven't been out with anyone since I moved here. You know I've been clean," she snarls.

"You can have Missy Friday after school, and you'll have her home by seven in the morning Saturday. The Derby is a no-go for you."

"You're such a stubborn ass!"

"Deal with it," I yell before I disconnect the line. I should feel bad, but I don't. She has kept up her end of the bargain where staying clean is concerned, but even after all this time, I still don't trust her. Nita says it's leftover feelings from before, but my gut doesn't believe it.

When I finish tossing out the hay, I ride over to Ethan's mom's place. The front door is wide open, and I'm greeted with Rose and Missy all dressed up wearing their hats.

"Don't you two look like something out of a Disney movie." I take off my bandanna and bow to them.

"Just like a princess." Missy curtseys.

"Momma is gonna want a million pictures of us," Rose says.

"You two need to go change for picking blackberries. You wouldn't want to ruin your dresses before the special day." I shoo them off.

"I'm glad they like them," Winifred says.

"Thank you. You didn't have to do that for them."

"Sure, I did. Ethan thinks of them as family, and that makes them mine too."

"Speaking of family, the old man says a lot of things he don't mean."

"You don't have to apologize for your father. I

know under all his gruffness there is a good man." She walks up to me, staring me in the eyes. "Do you know how I know that?"

I shake my head.

"Because he's raised some good children into fine adults."

"He'd say my mother was responsible for that."

"Poppycock. I see that ornery man in each of you." She points. "But I also see his goodness."

"Yeah, he's not so bad once you get through that thick head of his."

She sits in one of the chairs. "When Ethan left home for the military, he was a much different young man. He'd been spoiled, but he never acted like it. He was lost and wanted to find his own way in this world. Admittedly, I wasn't thrilled about his choice. Over the years, when he'd come home, I saw the boy before me growing into a young man. He still lacked his purpose, but he had changed. The way he walked, talked, and held himself was different. It wasn't until the last few years he'd been home for a visit that I saw the man he is now. He's grown up to be a fine young man. He became what he wanted, not what we wanted for him." She laughs. "Who knew it would be a cowboy." Tears fill her eyes but not from pain. "I'm so proud of him. I don't believe for one minute that your father didn't have a hand in guiding him. And, for that, I'm grateful. He helped him in a way his father and I never could. I owe him more than he'll ever know."

I sit on the arm of the couch next to her. "I've liked Ethan from the moment he came home with Clem. None of us ever knew he came from money until recently. He's worked hard and found his place on the ranch. When things got tough here, he could've bailed, but he didn't. He dug in harder to help us all out. I have so much respect for him. My old man may have given him something he was looking for, but you and your husband laid the foundation for him. He has only spoken of love and admiration for you. Don't give all the credit to my old man."

"What was your mother like?" She tilts her head.

"She was the backbone of this family. A true rancher's wife. This life ain't easy, but she never complained. She loved it and all of us. Including Ethan."

"We're ready, Grandma York," Missy says, running out of the room holding a basket.

"That sounds so pretentious. Why don't you call me Grandma Winnie?" She stands.

I laugh to myself, knowing my father will be downright pleased with himself.

"We have to be back by three, Grandma Winnie,"

Missy says. "Momma Sandy will be here to pick me up."

I squat in front of her. "There's been a change of plans. Something came up at the last minute, and she can't get you until Friday."

"Did she tell you I invited her to the Derby?" She cocks her head.

"About that, I told her to have you back early Saturday morning. You should've checked with me and Momma before you asked her. It's family only, sweetie."

"I'm sorry, Daddy. I'm sure she'd rather hang out with her new boyfriend anyway."

Sandy didn't mention a new man friend. "I'll talk to her about it on Saturday. You girls go have fun picking blackberries with Grandma Winnie."

CHAPTER THIRTEEN
JANE

"I'll be back around two to help with the check-in process," I say as I hit the bottom landing of the stairs.

Margret spins her chair to look at me. "Ethan's put a little pink in your cheeks," she says with a smirk.

"What did he say?" I storm toward her.

"Nothing at all. But I saw it in his eyes when he came downstairs. Besides, I've been at the front desk since seven, and he never came through the front door, which could only mean he spent the night." She turns back around to the counter.

"Please don't make a big deal of this. Neither one of us want the townspeople to know just yet."

"Know what?" Matthew comes up from behind me.

"Why pray tell are you still here?" I toss my arms in the air.

"Because you are." He stands next to me.

"I can have you thrown out of the Magnolia."

"And yet you haven't." He grins and tosses a tendril of my hair over my shoulder.

"I've been nice up until now. You and I are over! Get it! We"— I point between us—"will never get back together.

He gets down on one knee. "I'm sorry for the things I said to you. I was an idiot."

"Are you kidding me? Get off the ground!" I pull him up by his collar. "You're right. You were an idiot. But I'm thankful because if it weren't for your complete stupidity, I wouldn't be here now. Look around. This is my life, and I love it and the people in it. They accepted me when they had no need to. I was a complete stranger barging into their lives, begging for their help. Unlike you, they didn't kick me to the curb!" I turn in a circle. "I have a hankerin' to throw you out! And while I'm doing it, you can kiss my go to hell!"

Margret claps slowly. "Well, I s'wanee. It's about time you got the gumption to tell him off."

I chuckle at her southern slang. "She's right. I left Texas with my tail tucked underneath me and never had the chance to tell you how you made me feel. You showing up here, trying to win me back, is laughable." I press my finger to his chest.

"I'm not leaving." He thrusts his jaw in the air.

I drop my hand to my side. "Good."

He seems surprised by my answer. "So, you're giving me another chance?"

"I want you to stick around and see how happy I am here. How much I've grown and the things I've accomplished without you in my way."

His eyes fill with shards of anger. "I was never in your way. You forget that I was the one who encouraged you to become bigger than some poor little country girl who never knew her father. You didn't have a pot to piss in, much less a window to throw it out of. Those were your words, not mine. If it weren't for me, you'd still be living in a pathetic, run-down trailer park."

Before I realize how much he got to me, my palm connects with his cheek. His head turns to the right; then he flexes his jaw as he rubs it. "I guess I deserved that. Now we're even. If I can forgive you, then you should do the same. We can start over."

"Is he for real?" Margret touches my arm.

"Actually, he is. He's the same pompous bastard that dumped me when I needed him the most. He's always thought the sun comes up just to hear him crow. I was too blind to see it." I prop my hand on my hip so I don't slap him again.

Margret wheels between us. "I will fully refund your money. Get your things and get off my property."

"I'm not leaving until I get what I want."

"My wife asked you nicely to get your things and leave." Wyatt's baritone voice booms as he stomps into the foyer. Wyatt towers over him by several inches.

Matthew swallows hard, causing his Adam's apple to bob a few times. "I'll get my things and be out once I find another place in town to stay."

Wyatt steps within an inch of him, glaring down. "You do that, but if I hear that you've come anywhere near Jane or my wife, I'll hunt you down. There will be no body parts left to ship back to Texas."

Damn. Wyatt is fierce. I'm even trembling in my boots.

Without another word, Matthew stomps up the stairs.

Wyatt turns to face me. "If he comes anywhere near you, I expect my phone to ring."

I step on my tiptoes, placing a kiss on his cheek. "Thank you for your protectiveness. I love you for it, but I can handle him." I face Margret. "I'll be back later so you can spend some time with my niece and nephew."

"We love you," she says.

"I know, and I'm thankful every day for this family." I pat her hand and head out the grand entrance of the Magnolia Inn.

I call Molly on my way to my office and tell her about my run-in with Matthew.

"Good for Wyatt," she says.

"I don't want to see him dead, so I'm hoping he'll use the good sense his momma gave him and leave town."

"You don't still have feelings for him, do you?" Molly asks.

"Good lord, no, but I am grateful that he ended it with me, or I would've never come here. And being with the Calhouns has made me see that I never really loved him. He's not the type of man I would've ever been happy with. He's self-centered and only wants a woman that looks good on his arm."

"Unlike Ethan," she adds.

"Ethan is a true gentleman. Well, except for the whole naked thing." I can't help but smile.

"What?" She giggles.

"Never mind. I just pulled into work."

"You can't leave me hanging after saying something like that." She roars in laughter.

"I gotta go. Love you," I say, hanging up.

I know Ethan has not had enough time to go home and change, so he's not here yet. My insides are all giddy thinking about him. Last night was perfect. He let me have what I wanted, yet there was so much strength in him making love to me. It was give and take, not one-sided at all. He made me feel beautiful, inside and out. The way he took me in made me feel sexy. For the first time, my scar became part of me, not some hideous thing I wanted to hide. I rub my hand over it. I have a second chance in life because of it, and because of my old man. A man I'm proud to call father. I think about how wrong I was about him. I hated him growing up, not truly knowing both sides of the story. I think both my parents could've made better choices, but it's water under the proverbial bridge. I miss my mother dearly, but I'm so thankful something good came out of it by meeting him and all my siblings. Unlike Noah, it took me a bit to bond with all of them. Now, there isn't anything in the world I wouldn't do for each of them. They're my family, even with all their flaws.

I dig into work quickly, focusing on the topics from the councilmen. My assistant quietly comes in, placing a mug of coffee on my desk. I look up, acknowledging her but keep working. It's noon before I glance up and see Ethan standing in my doorway. He's dressed in blue jeans, a black belt, boots, and a denim shirt. His cowboy hat is gripped in his hand. What stands out the most is the gold badge clipped to his shirt that says, Livestock Agent.

"That looks good on you," I say. I feel as if I'm holding in drool over him.

"It does, doesn't it." He moseys into my office.

I glance at my watch. "You're a little late for your first day of work."

"I thought you weren't my boss." He chuckles.

"I'm not. I just thought I'd see you sooner." I rest back, crossing one leg over the other to stave off my ache for him even though I lost count of how many times he made love to me last night.

"Chet was in one of his moods. I had to clean out the barn before my mother tried to handle a pitchfork."

"He was going to put your mother to work?" I snicker.

"Something like that." He lays his hat on my desk.

"I think he likes her."

"He's got a funny way of showing it, but I think you're right."

"What's on your agenda today?" I sit up straight with my elbows on my desk.

"I have last year's numbers to review, and Boone is going to meet me here to introduce me to the buyers. We're taking them to dinner, so it's going to be a long day." He picks up his hat, placing it snuggly on his head.

"I'm only here for about another hour. I have to cover for Margret at the Magnolia this afternoon."

He walks around to my side of the desk, grasping my hands and pulling me to my feet. "How about I come to your place when I'm done."

"I would like that," I say, then take a step back when I hear footsteps coming down the hall. "Good luck on your first day as an agent," I say loudly, holding out my hand.

Bob steps into my doorway.

Ethan takes the hint, shaking my hand. "Thank you, Ms. Mayor. I appreciate your support and the opportunity to work for the town of Salt Lick." He lays it on thick.

He tilts his hat at Bob as he moves past him.

"Is there something I can do for you?" I ask Bob as I sit in my chair.

"I wanted to drop these files off before I head to the store. These are last year's tax numbers for the town. I thought you might want to take a gander at them before you start on the budget." He hands them to me.

"Yes. Thank you."

He stands still as if he has something more to say.

"Is there something else?"

"I wanted to apologize if I behaved in any way that offended you. I know I have a bit of a reputation, but I meant no disrespect to you."

"I appreciate the apology, Bob. What you do in your private life is your business, but I do expect you to be professional when it comes to any of the women working here."

"Understood, Ms. Mayor. It won't happen again."

"Then, all is forgotten." I smile. "Thank you for these files." I hold them in the air.

"You have yourself a good day." He tips his hat and marches out.

That was totally unexpected. Maybe I'm finally gaining their respect in my position. Wyatt left some tough shoes to fill. Being a woman, it hasn't been easy. Thus, why I need to keep my distance from Ethan at work. There is a fine line I have to walk, or everything I've built here could come crumbling down.

I review the files then tuck them into my briefcase to study later as I go back to the bed and breakfast. Margret seems a little frazzled with her normally perfect hair in disarray. She has a smudge of mascara under her eye as if she's been crying.

"You alright?" I ask, tucking my briefcase under the counter.

"Nothing for you to fret about." I hear a soft sniffle.

"I'm here if you need to talk."

"I'm fine. I'm going to go spend the rest of my day with my babies." She leaves without another word.

Margret has never once since the shooting felt sorry for herself. She was amazing the way she never let it get her down, but it has to be difficult. I wanted to do my part in helping her, and that's how I ended up moving into the Magnolia and working. I don't regret it for one minute.

"Where's Margret? I told her I'd pick her up at two." Wyatt holds keys in his hand.

"She just left out the back."

"Damn stubborn woman."

"What's going on? She looked like she'd been crying."

"I have this dinner planned tomorrow night with some of my old colleagues from New York who are passing through town. I offered to take her shopping for a new dress."

"I don't understand. Why would that upset her?"

"Your guess is as good as mine." He shrugs.

"I can stop by after work to try to make some sense out of it," I offer.

"I'd appreciate it. Every time I bring it up, she gets a burr in her saddle."

"That ain't like her. There has to be more to it."

"I agree but getting her to talk about it isn't easy."

"Margret!" I holler, opening the front door to her house.

"She's locked herself in the bedroom, and she won't come out." Her nanny points to the room.

"How long has she been in there?" I shut the door behind me.

"She came home, played with the twins, fed them a snack and said she had to find something to wear for Mr. Calhoun's dinner party tomorrow. Next thing I know, she locked the door, and I heard her sobbing. I've knocked, but she told me to go away."

I lean over, kissing the top of Amelia's head, who is playing with a stuffed animal. "Hey, pretty girl." Then I blow zerberts on Chase's belly. He grins like a possum eating a sweet potato. "You're a silly boy."

Making my way to the master bedroom, I walk softly across the wood floor.

"Margret, it's Jane. Will you let me in?" I tap on the door with my knuckles.

"I want to be left alone," she sobs.

"If you tell me what's going on, maybe I can help." She mewls louder. I jiggle the doorknob. The nanny taps my shoulder, handing me a credit card. Sliding it between the door, it opens when I turn the knob again. Pushing it slowly, I ease it shut behind me.

"Margret, I just want to help."

She lifts her head off the bed. In her true southern fashion, she sits. "I'm fine. I just needed a minute to gather my thoughts." Her mascara is streaming down her face.

I step over a pile of dresses to sit next to her. "What's all this?" I ask, regarding the dresses.

"Wyatt wanted to take me dress shopping," she cries, laying her head on my shoulder.

"Why is that upsetting you so much?"

"He wants to show me off." Her cries become gasps of air.

"Wyatt adores you. Why wouldn't he want to show off his beautiful wife?"

"At some point, he's gonna think me a burden." She leans over onto the bed, drowning out her bawling.

I get off the bed and onto my knees so I can see her face. I brush her blond strands of hair back until I can see her eyes. "Wyatt would never think you a burden. He loves you more than life itself. I know I haven't been around as long as the rest of the family, but Wyatt was immersed in himself before the two of you got together. Now he's as happy as a pig in sunshine. You and those two gorgeous children are his world."

"I'm never gonna walk again, and he's always gonna have to take care of me," she sniffs.

"You take care of each other. That's how this marriage thing works. Besides, you do pretty much everything on your own. You run a business and manage two happy babies."

She sits on the edge of the bed. "I have lots of helping hands to get through my day."

"We all do." I sit with her. "Do you realize how much you bring to my day? You're happy-spirited, and you're an impressive businesswoman. I learn from you all the time. There isn't anyone I respect more as a woman."

"Really?" She wipes her nose with the back of her hand.

"Yes, and I envy the relationship you have with Wyatt."

Her head falls to my shoulder again. "He never complains."

"That's because he's got nothing to whine about. The two of you love each other so much."

"That's just it. I want to be able to dance with my husband. Take long walks sharing our day. Twirl around in a dress he bought for me. Carry my children on my hip." She starts shedding tears again.

"Oh, sweetie, you are such a courageous woman. The only thing that matters to Wyatt is that you love him."

"I pictured our lives so differently."

I stand in front of her, lifting her chin in the air. "You and Wyatt wanted a ranch of your own. Done. You wanted to build the Magnolia Mill. Done. You wanted children. You got two." I hold up my fingers. "You wanted a man who would love you till death do you part. You have all of that and more. You not being able to walk hasn't changed any of it." I lean down, picking up a few of the dresses from the pile. "You're going to go wash your pretty face, put on some fresh makeup, and you and I are going shopping. We're going to pick out a sexy little number, and your husband isn't going to be able to keep his hands off you during dinner."

She giggles through her tears. "You think so?"

"I know it for a fact. So much so, that you are

going to surprise him by renting one of those cute new cottages on the edge of the town overlooking the river. It will be my treat. I'll stay here with the twins tomorrow night."

"I can't ask you to do that," she sniffs.

"You didn't ask. I want to do this for you. Besides, I don't get enough time with my niece and nephew."

She tugs me into a hug. "Thank you."

"No more feeling sorry for yourself. You have a beautiful life."

"You're right, I do."

"I'm going to pull the car around, and we're going to go have some fun."

I walk slowly until I hit the front porch, then I take off in a jog toward the Magnolia. Big fat tears roll down my face. I know exactly how Margret feels. I swore I'd never get married for the same reasons. What if I get sick again? I don't want to be a burden to the man I love. Her pain fills my gut. It was easy to be strong for her, but not when it comes to myself. I won't let down my walls for Ethan. He deserves a long, healthy life with the woman he marries. I can't promise that for him. My donor kidney could fail, or mine could. Not to mention the fact I can't give him a family. The way he looked at me and made me feel, I'd forgotten the reasons I kept him at bay. He wants so much more than I could ever give him.

Swinging open the entry door, I almost run into Wyatt.

"Hey, slow down. You alright?"

"I'm fine." I hide my heartache. "I'm taking Margret shopping."

"I thought I was taking her." He raises a brow.

"Change of plans." I try to move past him, but he grabs me by the arm.

"She isn't kicking me out, is she?"

I whirl around to look at him. "Why would you think such a thing?"

"I don't know. The past couple days, she's been distant. When I try to talk to her about it, she can't even look at me."

A couple comes down the stairs, heading for the door. I take Wyatt's hand, leading him into the office. "She's been feeling down about herself. She loves you so much and doesn't want her husband to become her caretaker. And, if you tell her I told you, I'll punch you in the face."

"That's nonsense. She takes care of all of us and then some."

"I know that, but she's feeling insecure."

"What can I do to help her through it?" He scratches his head.

"Just keep loving her like you do."

"I love her with my whole heart. Her not being

able to walk hasn't changed a thing. She's the most beautiful, kindhearted woman I know."

"Tell her that, every day." Who am I to give advice? I know nothing about marriage or love. "I gotta get changed." I motion to leave. "Oh, and you have a hot date with your wife after your dinner tomorrow night. I'm reserving one of the new cabins by the river for the two of you. What happens in that cabin is up to you. Make it a night she'll never forget." I run up the stairs to my room.

I READ A TEXT FROM ETHAN AS MARGRET TRIES ON a couple of dresses in the changing room.

I can't wait to see you tonight. The way things are going, I'm afraid it's going to be a late evening. Boone says these men we are meeting with are heavy drinkers.

I bite my lip as I respond. *I have an early day tomorrow. We'll have to get together another time.*

I wait for the three little dots to disappear. *Get together another time. You make it sound like a casual meeting. I think we are more than that.*

Gah, I don't want to hurt him. *We had our fun but being a couple would get in the way of my position as mayor. Please respect my decision.*

The three dots come and go several times, but no words follow.

"What do you think about this one?" Margret's voice has me looking up.

She's in a shimmery red dress cut low in the front, showing off her cleavage. "I'd say you have a winner. Wyatt will be falling all over you."

Her face lights up like a ray of sunshine bursting through the clouds on a rainy day. "I think he'll like it."

"I have no doubt." I giggle.

"Thank you for helping me today. You made me feel so much better. I want to repay you for all you've done for me."

I tap my finger to my lip. "I could use a piece of cherry pie from Nita's place."

"Done." She laughs.

I check my phone several times for a response from Ethan while Margret checks out, but there is nothing.

Holding the door open for Margret, we cross the street and down one block to the café. My father is sitting at a table with a classy-looking woman, chomping on a hamburger. I wave, and he motions for us to join them.

"Have you met Ethan's mom?" he asks.

"Oh, I've been meaning to stop by." I swallow hard.

"This is Wyatt's sweet bride, Margret, and this is Jane, Noah's twin sister."

Ethan's mom holds out her hand. "It is so nice to meet the two of you. Please join us."

She doesn't seem to relate me to Ethan at all. Maybe he hasn't told her about me.

"How are you liking the countryside?" Margret wheels close to the table.

"Not what I expected at all, but I can see why my son loves it here so much." Her gaze lands on me. "Chet has told me you're the mayor of Salt Lick."

"Yes, ma'am. Thanks to Wyatt. He made it happen."

"Let me guess. You two are here for pie. You know we serve all sorts of other food, right?" Nita laughs, placing water on the table.

I reach over, tapping the back of the empty chair. "Why don't you join us?"

She sits. "I do own the place." She smiles. She looks over her shoulder to a waitress. "Bring us a cherry pie," she says.

"What have you ladies been up to?" Daddy asks between bites of food.

"Jane and I have been dress shopping. Wyatt is taking me to dinner tomorrow night with a few of his friends from out of town, and thanks to Jane, we're having a romantic night at the cabins without children." She blushes.

"Good for you," Nita says. "You two deserve it."

"Chet has told me all about your two beautiful babies. I'd love to meet them." Mrs. York wipes her mouth with the edge of her napkin.

"The Kentucky Derby is Saturday. Let's say we all meet at the main house on Sunday. We haven't had a meal with the entire family in a while. It's time." Daddy isn't asking; he's telling. "I'll call Clem and have her let everyone know. She's good at that sorta thing."

"I'll man the bed and breakfast so Margret can attend," I say, trying to get out of it.

"You'll do no such thing. I'll get one of the women I've been training to take over for a few hours." She squeezes my hand.

"That's it then. Sunday at three. I'll expect everyone to be there." Daddy taps the table with the side of his fist.

My phone vibrates in my lap. I sneak a peek to see Ethan texted me back. *We'll talk later*, is all it says. Doggone stubborn man. Picking up my glass, I take a sip of water.

"You're the one my son loves," Mrs. York says, and I choke on my water.

"Don't go embarrassing her," Daddy says.

"I only want to get to know the woman who has won over my son's heart." She glares at him.

"Mrs. York..."

"Winnie," she interrupts, and my dad, for an unknown reason, breaks out in a deep chuckle. "Please, call me Winnie." She glares at him.

"Winnie, I have the utmost respect for Ethan, but I'd rather not discuss my relationship with him. We're good friends. Nothing more."

"He seems to think differently." Her soft eyes fill with some emotion. I don't think it's anger, maybe disappointment.

"Let the two of them work it out." My father comes to my rescue.

"Tell me all about the city." Margret touches my leg under the table. Ethan's mom fills our ears with New York and all her travels. She mentions Ethan often in her stories, and I can see how much she adores her son.

CHAPTER FIFTEEN
ETHAN

She liked the spanking. Maybe she'd prefer one when I'm angry with her. I hit Send, telling her *we'll talk later*. If I could leave this meeting, I'd head straight to her place.

"The first head of cattle will be ready to go to market in the next couple of weeks. Ethan will negotiate the terms, and from what I've seen him put on paper, I think all the ranchers in Salt Lick will be incredibly pleased," Boone tells the men sitting at the round table. The restaurant sat us in a room reserved for larger parties. One representative from each ranch in town is present. Boone is at ease with these men and vice versa. I think it will take some doing to get them to feel as confident with me.

"I've extensively researched the prices over the last couple of years. I believe we can do better."

Boone stands, handing out the files I prepared for each of them. "As you can see in the graph, I've come up with ways to save some money on our hay costs next year, along with reductions in the price of grain. I'll negotiate the terms with the locals that grow grain and corn."

"What makes you think they're going to reduce their costs to us?" Jim, who represents Cast Iron Ranch, asks.

"Because I've found additional buyers in the Pacific Northwest who are willing to pay a higher price for their goods because of the shortages they have with their locals shipping product overseas. If you'll flip to the next page, you'll see their potential increase in sales. I've already been in contact with their co-op."

"You work fast," one of them comments. "It's only your first day on the job."

"I can't take credit for all of it. Once I learned about this position, Boone and I started putting our heads together."

"Don't let him fool you. All I did was tell him where to look. He did all the leg work, and it only took him a few hours. I told you he would be perfect for the job." Boone pats me on the back.

For the next hour, I field questions, and we drink whiskey. Before I know it, there are ten empty whiskey bottles on the table. I enjoy a few glasses on occasion, but I've had more than my limit. I'm feeling it in my head.

"One more round," Jim says, raising his glass in the air.

Not really wanting it, I tip the square cup to my lips and down it in one swallow. I know I've had enough to drink because it doesn't burn as it goes down anymore.

One by one, they all stand after paying their bills. Jim walks over to Boone and me. "I think choosing you for livestock agent was a wise decision." He holds out his hand.

Focusing, trying not to see double, I meet his grip. "Thank you."

Boone chuckles. "I think it's time we call it quits. It's after midnight." Boone grips my shoulder, keeping me from stumbling. "Wait until they are all gone," he whispers.

I can feel my body swaying back and forth, and I have no control over it.

"Come on, I'll drive you home," Boone says.

"How do you do this? I'm not a big drinker." I hear my own words slur.

"You learn to cut it down with water in between." He keeps his hand on my shoulder, guiding me to his truck.

"I was going to Jane's place. Not mine," I say, opening the heavy truck door.

"Do you think that's a good idea, considering you're drunk?"

"I'll be fine by the time we get there."

"I'm not so sure about that, but you being alone ain't good either." He starts the engine.

"I'll be alright," I say, missing the button twice before I let the window down. The night air feels good but doesn't do much to sober me up. As soon as Boone pulls up to the Magnolia, I open the door, stumbling out. He puts it in park and jumps out.

"How about you let me help you."

I shrug him off then start unbuttoning my shirt.

"What are you doing?" He walks next to me as I trip on the first step.

I sit, pulling off my shirt, then start with my boots.

"Do you plan on taking off all your clothes?"

The two of him are squatting in front of me. "Jane has this thing about her scar." My words sound weird.

"I really think I should take you back to the ranch before you make a fool of yourself." He chuckles.

I hand him my shirt, kick off my boots on the landing and reach for the railing to stand. "I'm fine." I walk to the next landing and peel out of my jeans.

Boone takes out his phone and snaps a picture. "Clem is going to love this," he mutters.

When I come to Jane's room, I knock on her door with one hand, the other I'm dragging my jeans by one pant leg. "Jane, let me in," I say, trying to look through the peephole.

I hear her unlock the door and take a step back, bumping into Boone. He grabs my arm, holding me upright.

"What the hell?" Jane states, grasping her robe together.

"I tried to tell him this wasn't a good idea," Boone tells her.

"Why is he naked?" She yanks my jeans from my hand.

"I didn't want you to be embarrassed," I stammer.

"That makes as much sense as tits on a bull." She sounds angry.

"I think I either need to carry his ass home, or you need to let him inside before he wakes up all the guests." Boone shoves me inside when Jane steps aside.

"I think you should take him home." Jane crosses her arms, and I can see the swell of her breasts.

I falter over to her bed, plopping down. "I have no intention of leaving."

I fall back with my arms spread wide. I can hear

the two of them chatting, but I have no idea what's being said. The next thing I hear is the door closing. I lift my head to see Jane moving toward me.

"Hey, beautiful." I smile.

"Hey, nothing. I told you not to come over." She sits beside me, and I move to my knees in front of her.

Reaching down, I grab my pants she tossed on the floor. It takes me a minute before I can get what I'm after out of my pocket. "I love you, Jane Calhoun. Please marry me." My world is swaying.

"You're a drunken idiot." She pushes my hand away.

"Me being drunk doesn't change the fact that I want you to be my wife. You keep pushing me away, and I'm not going to let you."

"Stop," she says.

"Do you want me to spank you again?"

She shoves me back, and I fall on the floor. Before I can get up, she's on top of me, drilling her nail in my skin. "If you lay one hand on me in your drunken state, I'll kill you in your sleep, cut your balls off and toss them in your casket. Do you understand me?"

I gulp. I've never seen her so angry. I reach to touch her face, but I'm not sure which one is really her. "You're so pretty when you're mad." I sit, grabbing her around the waist.

Her body relaxes when she lets out a loud sigh. I move my hands to the front of her, pushing open her robe and kissing the spot of skin between her silky shorts and camisole top.

"Come on, let's get you to bed." She gets up.

"Now we're talking." I attempt to stand on my own.

"I'd say undress, but apparently, you did that in the hallway." She pulls back her tousled blanket.

I lie down, and she tucks me in, then walks over to the other side, taking off her robe. She climbs in, and I roll to my side. My eyelids suddenly feeling as if they are being weighed down.

My mouth is so dry. I lick my lips and tell her, "You're so damn gorgeous."

"So, you've said."

I can't keep my eyes open. She's talking, and every now and then, a word seeps in. Something about sick, and she won't put me through it. I have no idea what it all means. All I know is I'm curled up next to the woman I love.

❧

MY MOUTH IS FULL OF COTTON. I SMACK MY LIPS, trying to bring moisture to my tongue. One eye peels open, and I'm blinded by the sunlight coming in from the balcony.

"Balcony!" I shoot straight up. "Jane!" I holler, looking around the room. "Shit!" The clock blinks 9:05. I toss back the covers and pick my jeans up off the floor, tugging into them. "Where the hell are the rest of my clothes?" I get on the ground, searching under the bed. "What the hell." I stand on my knees, leaning on the bed, rubbing my temples. I see a piece of paper sticking out from under the pillow on the other side of the bed. Snatching it, I read it.

I HAD TO LEAVE FOR WORK. YOU WERE KNOCKED OUT cold, and I didn't want to wake you. Please don't be hurt by the things I told you last night, but you have to stay away from me. Please respect my decision. You're a great guy, and I wish I could give you what you want, but I can't. I won't. I put the ring on the nightstand. Save it for a woman who can give you everything you want. And, please, for god's sake, keep your clothes on when you're around me. Signed, Jane.

ME GETTING NAKED IN THE FOYER COMES RUSHING back to me, along with the fact I proposed to her again. "I'm such an idiot." I beat my fists on the bed.

"What did she say to me?" I think hard but don't remember her words.

Getting off the floor, I run into her bathroom to wash my face. I let the cool water seep in, hoping it will jar my memory. Drying my hands on my jeans, I feel the phone in my back pocket. Pulling it out, I scan over our texts. "I'll call her." I hold my finger on her name. "No, I have to see her in person."

Opening her door, I glance down the hallway first. Bare-chested and barefooted, I trod down the stairs.

Margret is behind the counter, talking on the phone. When she sees me, she finishes her conversation and hangs up. "Morning," she says, smiling cheerfully.

"Um, did you happen to find my boots down here?"

She rolls into her office then back out. "I think you might be missing a shirt too?" She all but giggles.

"Sorry, I had a little too much to drink last night," I say, taking my shirt and boots from her.

"Clem says she doesn't ever want to hear you razz her about her little Saran Wrap incident ever again."

My head falls, knowing there is more to the story. "How does Clem know what happened?"

She picks up her cell phone from the counter. "Boone captured the moment." She turns it in my direction, showing me the picture. Margret can't hold back her laughter. "Nice view, by the way."

"I hate him," I mutter.

"He said to call him when you needed a ride to your truck," she continues with her snickering.

"I'd rather walk." I storm out.

CHAPTER SIXTEEN
BEAR

"Where the hell is she?" I slam my phone on the table, cracking the screen.

"Calm down. I'm sure she'll have her home in a minute," Nita tries to soothe me.

"It's not like Missy to not answer her phone." I pace around the room. "Sandy promised to have her home first thing this morning. It's damn near nine o'clock."

"We've got plenty of time to make it to the Derby. We don't have to head out until noon. Boone and Clem took Moonshine last night."

"I know in my gut something is wrong." I snatch my keys from the hook by the front door. "I'm driving over to Sandy's place."

"I'll come with you." Nita grabs my phone, Missy's hat and dress and keeps step with me, racing for my truck. "I'll call Mike on the way and see if he's gotten any reports."

"I knew I should've never let Sandy back in her life." I slam the door and take off all in one move.

Nita buckles. "Maybe her car broke down, and they are stranded on the side of the road."

"For Sandy's sake, I hope so." My jaw hurts from clenching it so hard.

I burn through town and speed faster to the next town over where Sandy lives. I squeal to a stop next to her car. Running up the stairs two at a time, I beat on her apartment door. "Sandy! Missy!" I yell.

Nita tries to look in the window. "I can't see a thing. I don't think they're here."

"Then why the hell is her car out front." I pound, calling their names again. "Did you get ahold of Mike?"

"Yes. He didn't know anything. He said our next step would be to check the local hospitals."

Taking a step back, I strike out, connecting my boot with the door, smashing it open. "Missy!" I call again as I search each room of the small apartment. "Where the fuck are they!"

"I'm calling the hospitals." Her phone goes to her ear as mine rings. I almost drop it answering it. "Missy, is that you?" I say to the unknown number.

"My name is Peggy. I'm calling from a gas station a few miles east of Lexington."

"If this is a sales call, lady, I don't have time." I go to hang up but hear her say something else.

"There was a young girl here. She wrote on a bag of chips that she needed help. Your phone number is on it. She signed it, Missy."

"Was she hurt? Was someone with her?" I put it on speakerphone for Nita to listen.

"She looked like she hadn't slept, but she wasn't hurt. She was with a man buying beer. She kept saying she was hungry, and he yelled at her, telling her to grab a bag of chips. As he was paying, I noticed she was writing on the bag with a marker. She must've taken it off the shelf when he wasn't looking. He scolded her, telling her to hurry up. He stepped up to the window to look out and laid the bag in front of me. I quickly snapped a picture of it with my phone."

"How long ago did they leave? Did you call the police?"

"About five minutes ago. I'll call them as soon as I hang up."

"Send your exact location to this number. We're on our way."

We both run down the stairs, and as I'm getting behind the wheel, Nita already has Mike back on the line. She tells him what the lady told us.

"Do you know anything about Sandy's new boyfriend?" he asks.

"No. Nothing. I just heard about him from Missy the other day."

"Lexington is outside my jurisdiction, but I know the man in charge. I'll have him meet you at the gas station. Send me the address."

I try Missy's number again. "Come on, baby, answer the phone."

"We'll find her," Nita says.

"When I do, I'm going to kill the son of a bitch!"

"You have to calm down, or you're going to have a wreck." She holds on for dear life as the speedometer reads one hundred and ten.

I make the fifty-five-minute drive in thirty minutes after running several vehicles off the road. There are two police cars parked out front. I rush inside. "Did you find my daughter?"

"You must be Bradley Calhoun. Mike called me. I've got roads blocked off going toward Lexington. Can you provide me a picture of what your daughter looks like?"

Nita shows him on her phone.

"I'm sending this to my phone, so I can get it to my team of men."

"Peggy," I say to the women behind the counter. She nods. "Thank you for calling me."

"The cameras outside got a view of the license plate. We're running it now."

"Can I see the video?" I ask him.

He walks me into a back room with several screens lit up. "Luckily for you, the cameras are working. She said they had been down, but due to vagrancy in the area, they had them repaired two days ago."

He clicks a few buttons. "Here. You can see her walking back to the car. Do you know that guy?"

I indicate no with a shake of my head. "But I know the woman sitting in the passenger seat. It's Missy's mother. Sandy."

"Does she have custody of your daughter?"

"No, but she has visiting rights, and Missy has been staying with her every other weekend for about a year now."

"Has Sandy been in trouble before?"

"Yes. She's a recovering drug addict. She's been clean."

"Write down her name, address, where she works, and any known friends of hers." He hands me a notepad.

"I don't know any of her friends. The people she works with might know who she's been hanging out with." I jot down the information.

He steps away to make some phone calls.

"She must be terrified."

Nita wraps her arms around my waist. "She's a smart little girl. She found a way to tell someone she needed help. We'll find her."

It seems like hours have passed, but it was only moments before the sheriff is on his radio with one of his men, telling him they had identified the man that was with Missy.

"His name is Alex Strong. He's been in and out of trouble for years for his drug addiction."

"Shit!"

"He met Sandy at one of her recovery meetings according to one of the ladies she works with."

"Did you get an address on him?"

"He has multiple addresses on file. My men are checking them out."

"Any of them near here?"

"No."

I walk out to my truck and kick the tire. "Damn it!"

"Bear. Why don't you call Ethan and see what he can find? Maybe the guy has family around here?"

"That's not a bad idea." I pull my phone out of my pocket, getting Ethan on the line. I give him all the details, and he plugs them into his computer.

"This guy is a piece of shit. Not only has he been

in jail for drugs, he has pending rape charges and illegal possession of a handgun."

"Is there anything useful I can use to find where he might be headed?"

"Give me a second. I'm still searching."

I close my eyes tight, trying to be patient.

"His father owns a cabin in the mountains not far from Lexington. Ping me your location."

I do as he asks.

"It's three miles down the road from you as the crow flies. I'm sending you the address now."

I disconnect and motion for Nita to get in the truck. "Don't we need to tell the sheriff what you found?"

"There's no time for that." I jerk the truck onto the road, and in the rearview mirror, I see one of the police cars turn on its lights and start following me. Speeding down the road, I almost miss the turn on the dirt road. We bounce hard as I drive over the shoulder onto the road, and it dips down before I head in the right direction. It's backwoods, with lots of trees. I'm surprised Ethan was able to map me to it. We pass several run-down homes with no windows in them and barns that look like a light wind could blow them over. The road narrows, making a sharp turn, and I barely miss clipping a tree.

We round another S-shaped curve, and I see the roof of a house but no road to get to it. I slam on my brakes, take my rifle off its perch on my back window and get out, making the climb down. Nita is trying to keep up with me. When I make it to the yard, the car I saw in the gas station video is parked cattywampus in the grass.

"How the hell did he get down here?" I say softly to Nita.

"I don't know. I don't see a driveway. We should wait for the police to catch up with us."

I stop by a tree. "You stay here out of sight and wait for them. I'm going to find my daughter."

"Please be careful. Try not to get yourself killed."

"Out of sight," I say again, pointing at her.

I sneak up on the broken-down back porch and take a quick look inside. I see Sandy sprawled out on the couch. I'm not sure if she's sleeping or passed out.

Gripping the knob, I open it slowly, and it creaks in rejection. Alex rounds the corner. "Who the hell are you?" he shouts, aiming a gun in my direction.

"Daddy. I knew you'd find me," Missy cries, moving toward me. He reaches out and grabs her by the hair.

I direct my rifle at him. "Let her go, or you won't live to see tomorrow!"

He wraps his arm around her throat and squats behind her, pressing the pistol to her head.

"Daddy!" she cries again.

"It's okay. He's not going to hurt you." I raise my hands in the air.

"Throw your weapon on the ground," he says.

I bend down, laying it on the dirty carpet, kicking it toward him.

I don't let my eyes wander when I see Nita in the front window. She covers her hand over her mouth when she sees what's going on.

"Nobody has to die. She's a little girl. If you want to hurt someone, you can hurt me." I take one step closer.

"Step back!" he yells.

"What is it you want? Money, drugs? I'll get whatever you want. Just let her go."

Nita quietly opens the door. She has a fire log gripped in her hand. I take my wallet out and throw cash on the ground in front of him. "Here, I can get you more."

As he reaches to pick it up, I see multiple track marks on his arm. His eyes are dilated, and his hand has a slight quiver.

"How much more?"

"Whatever you want."

Nita creeps closer without a sound.

"You'll call the cops."

"No. All I want is my daughter, unharmed."

As he stands, Nita takes a swing, landing a hard hit to the back of his head. He stumbles forward, and I grab Missy, tucking her protectively into my body.

Alex reaches for the gun he dropped when he fell, and I push Missy to Nita. "Get down!" I wheel around, jumping on top of him. We wrestle for the gun, and it goes off. The bullet grazes my ear, and I hear Missy scream.

"Daddy!"

The back door crashes open, and the cops that followed us bust in, aiming their guns at Alex. He freezes, and I get one hard punch to his face before the cop pulls me off him.

They subdue him, handcuffing him.

"Are you okay?" Nita asks, and Missy runs into my arms.

"I was so scared," she cries.

As one cop drags Alex out, the other checks Sandy's pulse. He gets on the radio. "We're going to need an ambulance. We have a Caucasian woman, approximately thirty years old, unconscious. From the looks of her, she's a possible overdose."

I squat. "What happened?" I dry Missy's tears with my hands.

"He took us to a movie and took my phone, saying I could have it back when it was over. He made me sit in the row in front of him and Momma Sandy. When the movie was over, she was acting funny. She could barely walk to the car. He kept telling me she would be okay, but we were going to camp in the car for the night. I asked him for my phone, and he tossed it out the window. He parked in the woods, and when she woke up, he drug her outside. They were gone for a while, and I was so scared. It was dark out, and I couldn't see anything," she cries.

"It's alright, sweetie. You're safe now. Tell me what happened next."

"When he came back, he was carrying her in his arms. He tossed her inside like one of my rag dolls. He fell asleep as soon as he got behind the wheel. I got out of the car to try to run for help, but I couldn't. There were no lights at all. I got back in the car and closed my eyes. When I woke up, it was daylight, and he was driving. Momma Sandy would be awake for a minute, then out the next. I told him I had to pee, so he stopped at the gas station. He forced me to go into the boy's room so he could keep an eye on me. We went back into the store, and I saw a marker, so I picked up and started whining about how hungry I was."

"That's when you wrote on the bag of chips," Nita says.

Missy shakes her head. "I knew if I could ask for help, you'd come find me."

I hug her to me, kissing the top of her head. "You're such a smart girl and so brave."

She stays close by our side until the ambulance gets there, hauling Sandy off. I pick Missy up, carrying her up the hill to my truck. I open the back door, and Nita climbs inside with her.

I shut the door, and behind the darkly tinted windows, I retch. All the fear and emotions are knotted in my gut. I could have lost her today. I retch again. Once I regain my composure, I wipe my mouth on my sleeve and climb behind the wheel.

Nita looks at me in the rearview mirror with tears lining her eyes.

"Is that my dress for the Derby?" Missy says.

"Yes. But I'm sorry, sweetie, we're going to miss the Derby this year."

She sits up straight. "But Moonshine is counting on me to be there," she protests.

"I think you've been through enough for one day. I'm taking you home."

"Please, Daddy. I'm alright. I don't want to miss the race." She presses her hands together, pleading with me.

"I think we should go," Nita says.

"The police will want to talk to us."

"They can wait. Missy has been yearning for this day forever." Nita's stare is locked on me in the mirror.

Turning in my seat to look at them. "We should have her checked out first. Did he hurt you?" I ask.

"No, Daddy. Only when he pulled my hair." She rubs her head.

Against my better judgment, I give in to them. "Fine. We'll go to the Kentucky Derby. We're more than halfway there anyway."

"Thank you, Daddy." She curls into Nita's side.

CHAPTER SEVENTEEN
JANE

"This is so exciting. I've always wanted to come to the Kentucky Derby. Never in a million years did I think I'd do it with my family." I cling onto Molly's arm.

"Me either. I just love your hat."

"We look like royalty, don't we?" I giggle like a teenage girl.

"I don't know about that, but I'd love to peel you out of that dress when we get home." Noah's gaze eats her up.

"Gross, Noah. I don't want to hear what you want to do with my best friend." I plug my ears, and he laughs.

"Well, when your best friend happens to be my sexy wife, you'd better get used to it." He slaps her on the ass, and she yelps.

"Noah, behave," she scolds him through a smile.

"Where's Missy?" Rose asks Boone.

"I just got off the phone with them. They'll be here soon." I can tell by the deep-rooted scowl on his brow, something happened. I watch him whisper to Clem, and she all but gasps.

Margret wheels down the ramp to our area with Wyatt behind her. I've kept myself so busy the last couple days, I haven't seen them since the morning they came home from their night out.

"I didn't think you two were coming," I say, kissing her cheek. "How are things?" I ask softly.

"Couldn't be better." She reaches back, holding Wyatt's hand.

"Good. I'm glad."

Wyatt winks at me.

Ethan walks our way, grasping tickets in his hand. He smiles when he sees me, but it doesn't meet his eyes. I haven't seen him much either, other than passing at work. I made a point of not making eye contact with him when he came into my office with two of the ranchers wanting some information I had for them.

"He's looking mighty sexy." Molly elbows me.

Lifting my hand, I give him a small wave.

"Not as sexy as he looked in his boxers." She pokes fun at me.

"I can't believe Boone shared that picture with everyone." I squint at him and clench my jaw when he looks at me, smirking.

"Don't think for a minute it was my husband," Clem howls. "It's called payback for all the times you've made fun of Boone and I for our sexcapades."

"Well, if you two weren't so obvious about it, we wouldn't tease you," Ellie chimes in.

"Don't turn this on me. I wasn't the one running around in my boxers at the Magnolia," she protests.

"Could we not talk about it," Ethan says, his jaw firm. "My mother and Chet are headed in our direction, and there are children present."

"Don't you all look so nice," Winnie says, kissing Ethan on the cheek.

"Come sit by me, Grandma Winnie." Rose pats the seat next to her.

Chet walks directly over to Boone and drags him out of earshot. A few minutes later, Bear, Nita, and Missy come down the stairs. Bear looks as angry as his name. Missy runs to sit by Rose and Winnie.

Bear moseys over to the men, and Nita quietly tells us what happened.

"Oh my god. How is Missy?" Ellie asks.

"She seems okay. She insisted upon coming to the Derby."

"Have you gotten word on Sandy?" Margret asks.

"I called on the way here. She was pretty drugged up, but they said she would be fine."

"Bear will never let her see Missy again," I add.

"I know. I feel horrible for Missy. I want her to have fun today, and we'll deal with the fallout tomorrow," Nita says.

We all take our seats. Noah and Molly are in my row. I sit next to her, and Ethan sits beside me. My arm bumps his on the rest, and I place it in my lap. "Sorry," I say.

He boldly places his arm on the back of my chair.

"What are you doing?" I angle in his direction.

"Trying to get you to let me make things up to you."

"There's nothing to make up for."

"Then why won't you even look at me?"

"Ethan, I told you the other night, I can't do this with you."

The loudspeaker comes on, calling the trainers to line up with their horses. Boone kisses Clem, and we all wish him luck.

"Did you place your bet?" Ethan shows me his tickets.

"Of course, I did."

He moves close to my ear. "Look, I can't recall what you said. I was drunk and stupid. I should've just gone home. I'm sorry. I'd really like to know what you told me."

"We can talk about it but not right now."

"Can I get you a mint julep before the race starts?" he asks me.

"I'd like one," Molly says, leaning around me to answer him.

"I'll go with you." Noah stands, following Ethan to the bar.

"What's going on with the two of you?" Molly asks quietly.

"Nothing."

"Well, why not? You obviously like him, and he's madly in love with you."

"Some people just aren't meant to be together."

"You two are," she snorts.

"Please don't encourage him. He needs someone different than me."

"What's wrong with you, Jane?"

"Do you want the list?" I cock a brow at her.

"Whatever it is, it's all in your head. You're perfect for one another."

"I'm begging you to leave it alone," I say under my breath when the men return. "Thank you." Ethan hands me a glass. He has a bottle of water in his hand. "Didn't you want one?"

"Not after the other night."

We all settle into the announcement of each horse, their trainer, and the jockey. They parade down the field. Moonshine's number draped under his saddle is orange with a large number seven displayed on it in blue. Boone looks like a proud papa walking alongside him.

Missy getting up and moving past family in her row to get into Bear's lap, distracts me for a moment. She's a tough cookie, but she's still a little girl at heart. I'm not sure how Bear and Nita will handle her trauma, but I know we'll all be there for her.

The trainers leave the horses' side as they start the final lineup in their gates. Boone makes his way back to our seating area and stands in the back row. Clem joins his side for a show of support. I've never seen Boone look so nervous. His jaw flexes several times, and his Adam's apple bobs as he swallows hard several times.

The crowd roars as the horn blows, opening the gates. Moonshine is in the third row from the inside. The jockey has him digging in hard and fast, running in second. He maintains his position as they round the first curve of the track. We all cheer him on. Rose is bouncing up and down in her seat. I can feel her excitement beating inside me.

In the far stretch, the horse in third place is inching up on Moonshine. The horse in first place leads by a few strides. When they make the final turn toward the finish line, Moonshine's jockey leans his body closer to him and Moonshine darts forward, passing the first horse with the third on his tail. They are neck and neck for the last quarter mile. The finish line is in sight. We all rise, shouting to Moonshine.

The jockey maneuvers again. Moonshine crosses the finish line a full body length in front of the other horse, which comes in second. The crowd erupts.

Boone has his arms raised in the air. Clem is jumping up and down beside him. Missy leaves Bear's lap, running straight into Boone's arms.

"We did it! Moonshine won!" she cries.

She has tears of happiness mixed with heartache rolling down her little cheeks. She clings to Boone for dear life. Bear and Nita make their way toward her. For a solitary moment, they surround her as one protective family.

Moonshine is pronounced the official winner of the Kentucky Derby over the intercom. Boone carries Missy down to the track with Clem proudly by his side. A bed of red roses is draped between his neck and the jockey. Moonshine makes his final showing as the jockey waves to the crowd as he's being interviewed.

Boone stands on the sideline with his interviewer. I can't imagine what is racing through his mind. The winning payout is over one million dollars. Whiskey River Ranch will never need money again. All the years of hard work, early mornings, and late nights have finally paid off for him.

We collectively turn in our bids, cashing them out, and head toward the stalls where we know we'll find Boone and Clem. Ethan walks beside me, locking his pinky finger with mine. I know I keep telling myself I can never give him what he needs, but even his slight touch sends sparks through my body. I can't deny how much I genuinely want him. He grins, feeling it too.

We round toward the row of stalls, and Ethan pulls me to the side, letting the others pass. Fully grabbing my hand, he drags me between two barns, pushing my back against the wall, trapping my mouth in a sweet kiss.

"I'm sorry I got drunk and came to your place the other night. It wasn't my finest moment, but I wanted to be with you. I want you to be my wife, Jane."

I weave my hands to his chest. "I won't marry you, Ethan. I don't say that to hurt you but to save you from me."

"I don't want to be saved from you." He takes a

step back. "But I won't ask you again. I've made my feelings known. The rest is up to you."

"Why does it have to be all or nothing? I love the time we share together, even if it's only stolen moments."

"I want more," he states matter-of-factly.

"Can we please talk about this later? I'll come to your place."

He inhales deeply and nods. "I can't turn off my feelings for you, so don't expect me to."

"I don't want you to." I'm being completely self-ish. At some point, I'll have to love him enough to truly let him go. I take his hand, and we join our family in celebrating Moonshine's win.

CHAPTER EIGHTEEN
BEAR

"It's been a while since you and I've been able to steal away and have afternoon sex," I say as I zip up my blue jeans.

"I'm glad Boone covered for you so you could meet me for a quickie." Nita tugs the soft white sheets up to cover her bare breasts.

"I didn't exactly ask his permission." I chuckle.

"Hey." She grabs my hand. "I have something I want to tell you." Nita smiles.

I sit next to her. "Be quick, wench," I tease, smacking her ass and placing a quick kiss to her swollen lips from me devouring them.

She gnaws the inside of her cheek.

"You're starting to worry me." I stroke her dark hair.

"Nothing bad." She sits. "Actually, I think you're going to be very happy."

I yank down her sheet and straddle her, pinning her hands above her head. "What we just did made me very happy."

She wiggles her hips beneath me. "What do you think about another Calhoun running around the house?"

Releasing her hands, I slide down her body, pressing my lips to her stomach. "We're having a baby?"

I glance up, and she nods frantically with a grin covering her face. "Yes."

I lay my ear to her tummy. "Gawd, I love you."

She wiggles her hips again. "Does this mean you're happy?"

Raising up on my hands, I move back up her body. "The happiest man alive."

"I love you, Bear. You're a good man and a fantastic father. This baby will be the luckiest boy alive."

"Boy?" I raise my brows.

"I hope so. I want to give you a son."

I roll off her, lying on my side, propping up on my elbow. "I have to do a better job of protecting this one."

She joins me on her side, facing me. "You did

what you thought was best for Missy. She's a tough little girl like the rest of the Calhoun women. She'll be alright."

"I don't know how to tell her she can't see her mother again."

"The courts are going to have to decide that for you." She brushes her fingers through my hair.

"I will never trust Sandy again with our daughter."

"I know."

A knock on the door has me climbing out of bed. "That's probably my old man bringing Missy home." I throw a T-shirt on and head for the front door. "I didn't think it was time..." I stop mid-stance when I open it and find Sandy on the other side. She looks like shit. Her hospital band dangles from her arm. "You're one brave woman to show your face on this property. You can't stay. Missy will be here any minute."

"I saw her at the main house with your father. They were sitting on the front porch swing eating ice cream, so I knew she wouldn't be here."

"What do you want, Sandy?" I fill the frame with my body and my arms crossed over my chest, not allowing her one foot inside the house.

"How is she?"

"Fine, no thanks to you and your boyfriend. He

won't be getting out of jail anytime soon. You should be locked up with him."

"If it makes you feel any better, I lost my job."

"It doesn't," I say, gruffly.

"May I come in, please?" Tears fill her eyes.

Nita's hands wrap around my waist. "Let her say what she needs to say so she can be gone before Missy gets here."

I reluctantly move aside, opening the door wide and letting her walk inside. She sits in the single chair across from the couch. Nita takes a seat on the couch, and I grip the back of it, standing behind it.

"I know I screwed up." Her lip quivers. "I need you to tell Missy that I'm not coming back. I don't want to keep doing this to her. You were right, thinking I'd never stay clean. I don't know how to beat this beast. Lord knows I've tried. I'm going back into rehab, but I won't be coming back here to make false promises to our daughter again. I love her too much to keep hurting her. I'm so sorry," she sobs. "I would never leave if I thought I'd stay clean the rest of my life."

"You should've never come back in the first place," I bark. Nita tilts her head up and glares at me.

I raise my hands in the air. "Sorry."

"No, I deserve every ounce of anger you have

toward me. Because of my stupidity, our daughter could've died."

"I will find a way to tell her so that she'll understand."

The door flies open, with Missy and my dad marching inside. Missy grips her grandpa's hand when she sees Sandy. "I didn't know you were coming over," she says.

"Do I need to get my shotgun?" Dad grumbles.

"No." I move to his side. "Thanks for bringing her home." I motion my head toward the door, hoping like hell he'll take the hint without a fuss.

"Fine," he snarls, then points at Sandy, "but don't go thinking you're welcome on this property."

I shut the door behind him and squeeze Missy's shoulders. "Sandy has something to tell you." I walk with her to sit beside Nita, who she clasps on to.

"I don't want to talk to her," she says.

Sandy moves out of the chair onto her knees, crawling until she's directly in front of Missy. "I don't blame you. I'm so sorry for what I did to you. I'm an awful person and a terrible mother, but I love you. So much so that I'm not coming back. I don't ever want to put you at risk again. I know you are safe and loved here with your daddy and Nita." She looks up at Nita. "She's the type of mother I wish I could be."

"Why can't you change?" Missy stares at her.

"I tried, baby girl. Believe me, I tried. I can't promise to change. I wish I could." Her hand trembles as she raises it to touch the side of Missy's head.

I'm surprised when she lets her. "Will I ever see you again?"

"Maybe one day when you're older. I promise I'll try every day until then to get better."

"Can I write you?"

"I would love that if it's okay with your momma and daddy." She glances up at us.

Nita squeezes my hand on her shoulder, and I nod.

Missy slides off the couch and into her arms. Sandy's tears fall into her hair. "I'm so, so sorry."

"I love you, Mommy Sandy."

My eyes well up at Missy's words. Children are so much more forgiving than we are. My heart hurts for her, yet at the same time, I'm filled with pride.

After a long weepy moment, Sandy lets go of her and stands. "As soon as I'm out of rehab, I'll write you to let you know where I am," she says to me. She sniffs, wiping her nose on her sleeve.

Nita and I walk her to the door. "Don't let her down again by not writing her back."

"I won't."

I think she takes Nita by surprise when she hugs

her neck. "Thank you for doing what I couldn't. She adores you."

"Thank you for giving her to me," Nita whispers.

She lets go and moves through the door. Missy pushes her way between us, waving at Sandy. "I'll see you again someday," she says.

I shut the door and squat in front of Missy. "I'm so sorry she hurt you, but she's doing the right thing. She needs long-term help, and I love her for admitting it."

"May I go play in my room?" Her tiny lips quiver, holding back her tears.

I stand, kissing the top of her head. "Sure, you can. I'll come check on you in a bit."

She runs off, closing her bedroom door behind her.

"She'll be okay." Nita wraps her arms around my neck.

"Thank you for loving her like she's your own child."

"I promise to love her every bit as much as this little one." She glances down between us.

"One of the best days of my life was catching a car thief." I chuckle. "I love you." I kiss her sweetly. "I know I said I'd check on her, but I really need to get back to work."

"I'll do it. I kinda feel like crawling in the tent with her and playing Barbies anyway." She giggles.

"I'll try not to be late." I put my hat and work boots on before I open the door. "Hey. Does anyone else know about the baby?"

"Only you, me, and the doctor."

"Good. I want us to tell my family together after we tell Missy."

"I promise to not say a word, but don't make me wait too long. I'm busting at the seams to tell Ellie."

I drive the four-wheeler to the barn, and Boone is standing outside talking to Daddy.

"Everything alright?" Boone asks.

"I hope you ran her off for good," Dad says.

I drag my hat off my head. "Actually, she made the decision all on her own not to see Missy again."

"How's my granddaughter handlin' it?" he asks.

"Nita says she'll be fine in time. We'll keep a good eye on her."

"I'm sure you will." Boone slaps my back. "You're a good dad."

"Thanks, man."

"Enough of this shit. You two have work to do." Dad points at us.

"Won't hurt you to stay and help." I chuckle.

"I have a date with my recliner and Scar."

"I thought you didn't like that dog." I laugh.

"I don't." He winks. "Ethan's at his mother's house taking care of a few repairs, and the damn rat is shaking like a leaf. She asked if I'd come get her." He walks off.

"I think he likes the dog and Winnie." Boone elbows me.

"It'd be nice to see him happy again, but he and Winnie are worlds apart, and I don't think she would put up with his shit." I put my hat back on.

"Don't be so sure about that." Boone grins.

CHAPTER NINETEEN
JANE

"I swear, the man won't leave me alone." I turn off my cell phone.

"Who, Ethan?" Margret scowls. "I thought you liked him."

"Not Ethan, Matthew. He's texted me nearly a hundred times he wants to see me."

"I thought he left town."

"No. He's staying at the Rosebud Inn."

I grab my purse from under the counter. "I'm going to go take care of this once and for all."

"It's about time you quit going around your ass to get to your elbow. You should've sent him packing the first time he showed up at the Magnolia Mill." She wheels herself beside me to the front door.

Wyatt comes through it before I can let myself out.

"Hey. What are you two up to?"

"No damn good," I snarl, storming past him.

"Who licked the red off her candy?" I hear Wyatt ask Margret. I laugh to myself, thinking he's finally not such a fuddy-duddy. Margret has rubbed off on him with her southern ways.

I climb in my car and head straight for the newly updated Rosebud Inn. Other than the Magnolia, it's the nicest place in town. Only the best for Matthew. I park by the diner and walk two blocks down to the inn. I spot Matthew coming out of his room. He's locking the door as I come up behind him.

"What in all-fire hell is so important that you blew up my phone?" I ask, placing my hands on my hips.

"I was just headed out to find you. You never answered any of my texts." He unlocks the door, holding it open.

"I ain't staying long." I bump his shoulder as I stomp inside.

"I'm glad you're here. I want to discuss our relationship with you."

I whirl around. "You and I don't have a relationship." I use air quotes.

He pulls out the chair at the small round table. "Please have a seat and hear me out."

I begrudgingly sit. "You have five minutes."

"I realize how badly I treated you after I found out you were sick. I was a fool."

"Asshole is more like it," I snicker.

"Okay. I deserve whatever name you might call me." He paces the small area. "I'm a changed man. It took you leaving for me to realize how much I love you and need you in my life."

"Was that changing done before or after I came home to find some woman's long legs wrapped around your ass in my own bed?"

He pulls out the other chair, sitting. "I was in a bad place when you broke the news to me. I knew there was something wrong weeks before when you were too tired to have sex with me. A man has needs, and you weren't fulfilling mine."

"So, you thought it would be alright with me if you found another woman to meet your so-called needs." I slap the table. "What about what I needed? A man who loved me through my illness. You were so preoccupied with yourself, you never thought about what I was going through!" I yell, finally letting my anger for him out.

He raises his hands in surrender. "You're right. I know that now."

I stand. "Look, this conversation is pointless. I don't want you back. In fact, I want you to leave town today and never show your face here again."

"You don't mean that." He's on his feet. "I know we can make this work."

"I don't want you, nor do I love you anymore. I'm not sure I ever did."

"It's because of Ethan, isn't it?" His expression hardens.

"Yes, and I'd be an idiot to lose a man like him."

"Does he know you can't give him children?" He grabs my arm. "Because I'm willing to accept it."

"Let go of me!"

"You should tell the man and see if he loves you enough to stay with you."

"He's a good, honest man. Nothing like you."

"Still, a man wants a son to carry on his name."

A knock on the door has me opening it. "Ethan," I gasp.

Matthew wraps his arms around me, pulling me into his chest. "I'm glad he's here so you can tell him we're back together."

I elbow him hard in the stomach, knocking the wind out of him. "Get your hands off of me!" I yell, turning to look at him. When I whirl back around, Ethan is stomping off in the direction of his truck.

"Ethan! Wait! It's not what you think." I catch up with him before he opens the driver's side door.

"I didn't come here to interfere with you and your boyfriend," he seethes.

"He's not my boyfriend. Why did you come here?" I demand.

"To tell him to leave you alone and get the hell out of Salt Lick!"

"I came for the same reason."

"She's lying. She came here to beg me to take her back." Matthew runs up behind me, holding his side.

"What the heck is wrong with you!" I scream.

He grabs me by the waist, gripping me tight to his body. "I'll tell him your secret if you don't make him go away," he whispers sharply in my ear.

I grind my teeth, turning in his arms. My own words gut me. "I'm sorry, Ethan. He's right."

His jaw flexes back and forth, and his eyes darken. "I won't play second to anyone ever again." He gets in his truck, slams the door, and skids on the pavement as he races out.

I turn around, slapping Matthew hard across the face. "I hate you!"

He rubs his jaw. "That isn't any way to talk to your future husband."

"I will never marry you." I step up nose to nose with him. "If you aren't out of town by tomorrow, I'm going to let Noah escort you out. And just in case you missed what I'm threatening, you'll have a bullet between your eyes by the time he crosses the county line."

He gulps, knowing darn good and well Noah would do it.

"Your choice. You can leave dead or alive. Don't matter either way to me." I shrug. "Don't think for one minute you're going to go anywhere near Ethan again. I'll shoot you myself." I run to my car. I turn on my phone, and the first person I call is Noah. He tells me he'll make sure Matthew is out of town by tomorrow. The second number is Ethan's.

"Come on, pick up the phone," I say, tapping my steering wheel. I can't believe I hurt him like that. I wasn't ready to share my secret with him. The only reason Matthew knew was I told him out of anger. I wanted to hurt him, so I told him I did it, so I'd never have his children. I was in such a bad place when I found him screwing around.

My car bolts forward as I hit the pothole turning onto Whiskey River Road. I don't let it slow me down until I come to a skidding stop in front of the main house. I don't exactly know what I'm doing here. I need to find Ethan.

My shoes smack hard on the steps, and the screen door hits the wall as I throw it open. I stop dead in my tracks when I see Daddy sitting in his recliner in his tighty-whities with Scar nestled in beside him on the arm of the chair.

I cover my eyes. "Why are you in your underwear in the middle of the day?"

"My house. I have every right to be naked if I want. Maybe you should try knocking before you come busting inside my house." I see him rub his mustache when I peek through my fingers.

"Please go put some clothes on. I really need someone to talk to."

He stands. "Here, hold Scar, so she doesn't follow me up the stairs."

I take her from him and cover my eyes again.

He stomps up the stairs and returns fully dressed a few minutes later, thank god.

"What's got your knickers all in a knot?"

I hand him the dog. "That man lies like a no-legged dog!" I plop onto the couch.

"Who you talkin' about?"

"Matthew."

"What did he do to you?"

"You mean today or when I was in Texas?"

He sits next to me. "Both. You ain't ever given me any details."

I let out a long sigh. "After I found out I was sick, the man didn't want me anymore. He didn't want to have to take care of me. Worse yet, I found him in bed with another woman in my own home."

"I can shoot him for you."

"I appreciate it, but he's leaving town for good. Noah is making sure of it."

"So, what happened today?"

"I went to where he was staying at the Rosebud Inn to tell him to leave town. That he and I were never getting back together."

"Why do I have the feeling there is more to the story?"

"Ethan showed up." I rest my head on his shoulder.

"And he got the wrong idea."

"Sort of."

"Girl, you are as confusing as a fart in a fan factory."

"Matthew knows something about me that I haven't shared with Ethan, and he said if I didn't get rid of him, he'd tell him."

"I knew you were a true Calhoun. Who'd you kill?"

"Nobody. Don't go gettin' all excited. It's nothing like that."

"Are you going to tell me what's so awful?"

I cover my face and sob like a little girl. "I can't ever have children. The drugs were so harsh on my body, that they told me that I could die if I ever got pregnant. I made the choice myself. I was so afraid and fighting to live that I didn't think it would ever matter."

"You seem to be under the impression that Ethan wouldn't love you if he knew."

"I've heard him say so many times that he wants to be a father."

"I think you underestimate him. The boy fell in love with you the minute you moved here. I saw it written all over his face. He fought it for a long time because of his relationship with Ellie. He was a boy when he moved here, and I've watched him turn into a fine young man. He was an honorable man and stepped away from Ellie as soon as Ian came back. He saw how much they loved one another. I think it's taken him some time to admit he loves you."

I sob harder. "He's asked me to marry him several times, and I said no."

He tucks his arm around my shoulder. "And why is that? Just because you can't have babies?"

"Yes. No. I'm an idiot."

"Do you love him?"

"Yes."

"Then I'd say you have some wallering to do."

"You love my son?" We both look over the couch, not hearing Ethan's mom come into the house.

I rise. Wiping the tears from my face. "I'm sorry," I say.

She picks up Scar, who's been lying at my dad's feet. "Sorry for what? Loving Ethan?"

"No. For hurting him."

"I guess Chet is right. You need to make it up to him. At least I think that's what he said." She smiles.

"I don't think he'll forgive me."

"My son is a very forgiving man, especially when he loves someone."

"He's told you he loves me?" I sniff.

"Not in so many words, but I see it in his face at the mention of your name."

I turn in a circle twice. "I've got to find him."

"Good thing I know where he is. You might want to go wash your face first." She points.

I rub my cheek, and black mascara comes off in my hand.

"You need to come up with some kind of romantic gesture to help things along," Daddy pipes in, and I giggle.

"Romantic? Coming from you, I would never have believed it if I hadn't heard it with my own two ears."

"I still have some tricks up my sleeve." He winks at Winnie.

"He'll never ask me to marry him again."

"Then you best do the asking," Daddy replies.

"I have something that may persuade him." Winnie hands Scar to my dad. She unclasps a silver necklace from around her neck and slides something off it. "Here," she says, grasping it in her hand.

I hold mine out, and she drops a silver wedding band into it. "What's this?"

"It was my husband's. I can't think of anything better to give to my son. It will let him know I approve."

I hug her neck. "Thank you so much."

"I do approve, but if you hurt him again, you and I are going to have some harsh words."

I let go of her. "I won't. I promise."

CHAPTER TWENTY
CHET

"That was mighty sweet of you to do." I take Scar from her and sit in my recliner.

"You act surprised," she says, flattening her hair down.

"You've surprised me on many levels since you've been here. You being all big city, I figured you tuck your tail and run as soon as you saw this place."

"I have to admit, it was a bit of a culture shock." She sits on the couch. "It's grown on me. Don't get me wrong, I miss the city and the street sounds. That rooster of yours, I'm ready to find it a new home."

She laughs, and I like the sound of it. She's pretty, and she has a twinkle to her blue eyes. I like having her around.

"Are you going to make this your permanent home? I mean, I know it was only originally for six months." I clear my throat. "You're welcome to stay as long as you like."

"You surprised me too." She glances at her hands clasped in her lap. "I expected you to be..." She taps her lip.

"Ornery," I finish her thought.

"I'm not saying you're not, given the situation, but you can also be very sweet."

"Don't go spreading that rumor. I have a reputation to keep." I point at her.

"Your kids already know it. Take Jane, for instance. She came here to talk to you. From what Ethan has told me, she hasn't opened up very easily, and Noah's been the only one she confides in."

"She and I have bonded over time. I regret missing out on having a hand in raising her and Noah."

"Ethan told me what you did for her."

"I'm glad it was me. At the time, I didn't know if she'd ever want to be part of this family, and it was the only thing I could do for her. She's my daughter as equally as Ellie and Clem. Ellie's more of a pain in the ass." I chuckle.

"Like her father." She smirks.

I stroke Scar's furless body. "I even kinda like this one."

She stands, walks over to me, leans down and

kisses my cheek. "You're a good man, Chet." My gaze follows her into the kitchen, where she pulls down a glass from the cabinet.

I set Scar on the ground, and she runs to Winnie's side. "I'll have whatever you're fixing," I say, moving to the table.

She pours two glasses of tea, placing one in front of me, then she slides into a chair.

I stare at her for a moment. "Did you and your husband have a good relationship?"

She chokes on her drink with my question. "Why do you ask?" She takes a napkin from the center of the table, wiping her mouth.

"Curious. That's all."

"We did. Not to say we didn't have a few difficult years. When we first got married, he worked all the time. He was trying to build his business, so he was hardly ever home. There were times I thought he loved it more than me."

"Was he ever unfaithful?"

"I had my suspicions with him and his secretary. She was beautiful and smart. She hung on his every word."

"Did you ask him about her?"

She takes a long sip of her drink. "He had a long weekend away from home. He and I had been fighting a lot about him working so much. When he left, I was angry with him and he with me. Something was different when he came home on Sunday. He was more loving and thoughtful. He was home every night that week around six, which was very unusual for him. He had a look of guilt in his eyes I'd never seen before." She takes another sip. "I decided I'd surprise him at work on Friday with lunch. I was shocked when I was greeted by a new secretary."

"That don't sound too good to me."

"When he saw me, the look on his face said it all. He knew I knew."

"What did you do?"

"I decided in that split second to not speak of it. I kissed him, and we had a lovely lunch together."

"My Amelia would've said, 'don't let the screen door hit ya where the good lord split ya.'"

She busts out laughing. "I'm not sure what that means other than she would've thrown you out."

"She'd of picked up my shotgun on the way out and used it too." I laugh.

After we both stop laughing, I lean my elbows on the table. "How was your relationship after that?"

"He was a good father and a loving husband. I don't regret forgiving him for one minute. I think sometimes in life, we all need a pass. Isn't that what Amelia did for you?"

I take a deep breath, sitting back, rubbing my

chin. "The situation was a little different, but I suppose she did. She gave me more than one. I don't know if you've noticed or not, but I'm not an easy man."

"Something tells me Amelia knew how to handle you just fine."

"She was the love of my life. I wasn't the best husband, but I couldn't have asked for any better wife and mother to our children."

"Do you ever stop missing her," she sniffs.

I reach over and take her hand that's resting on the table. "I miss her every damn day, but time takes away a little of the ache, especially when I see her in my children. Wyatt reminds me the most of her personality-wise, but Ellie is the spitting image of her momma."

"Ethan resembles my husband's side," she says.

"I see you in him. He's a good man." Scar jumps in my lap. "Jane may seem a little messed up, but Ethan would be lucky to have her and she him."

"I only want my son to be happy."

"What about you? Do you think you'll ever find happiness again?"

"I'm too old to think such things." She looks away.

"I'd hate to think that about either one of us. I know this ranch, the land, my children, keep me busy, but it'd be nice to have someone to share the rest of my life with."

"Me too," she whispers. "I need more time to mourn my husband."

I stand, handing her the dog. "You take all the time you need. I ain't going anywhere." I mosey outside and to my truck. I drive to the piece of land Amelia is buried on, stopping in a field to pick a few flowers.

I lay the flowers on her headstone. "Hey, sweetheart," I say, looping my fingers in my belt. "Sometimes, it seems like just yesterday you left me. Other times, it's been far too long." I squat. "I miss your sweet, sweet smile. More than anything, I miss lying next to you."

I take off my Stetson and lay it on the ground next to me. "I'm sorry I haven't been here more often to keep you updated on the kids. Wyatt bought his own ranch. Can you believe that? Wyatt, a cowboy." I chuckle. "You were right about him and Margret all along. They are married and have two toddlers running around. Chase and Amelia. She has your eyes."

"Ellie, well, she's Ellie. What can I say? I never thought in all my years I'd see her as a mother. Ian's been good for her. Of course, you knew that too. They have a son, Deacon. He's the spitting image of his daddy. Let's just hope he gets his demeanor too." I laugh.

"Bear and Nita are good, but boy does Missy miss you every day. She repeats things that you taught her all the time. Don't you worry, she and I are still taking care of your chickens." My eyes start to water.

"Clem and Boone are happier than I've ever seen them. I told you about Rose last time I was here. She's as sweet as a peach. I think Clem has resigned herself to not having any more children. She loves Rose like she was her own flesh and blood, and that's enough for her. Boone finally won the Kentucky Derby with Moonshine. You would've been so proud of him."

I clear the lump in my throat. "I told you all about Noah. He married a fine young lady, Molly. She was as wild as a June bug on a string when he first met her. They are as opposite as can be, but it seems to work for the two of them. Then there's Jane. I've worried about her since the day she landed on my doorstep. She's as pretty as a pumpkin and smart as all get out. She don't like to show it, but she's vulnerable on the inside. She's scared to get too close to anyone. I'm supposin' that came from her being ill. She didn't expect to survive. She's been tiptoeing around Ethan the entire time, afraid of what she feels for him. I think she's finally figured it out. I just hope it ain't too late for the two of them. Ethan has grown into a man I admire. He's a hard worker and quick as a whip. If they can settle things down between them, they'll be as good as peas and carrots together."

I adjust to my knees. "That brings me to why I'm here." I swallow hard, and my throat goes dry. "Ethan's brought his mother here to live. Her husband died not long ago. She's a bit snooty at times, but she's come around. You'd like her very much, as I do. Her ugly dog has even grown on me. I'm tired of being alone, Amelia. I've loved you for as long as I can remember. I will never have a love like ours, but I could love again. We never talked about whether or not you'd want me to move on because, let's face it, we both thought I'd be gone long before you. The thought of you with another man would've killed me, but you were too damn sweet to be left alone for too long. I would want you to be happy. I'm not saying I'll win Winnie over, but when she's ready, I'd like to try and know that you're okay with it."

I touch her name on her headstone. "You were a good woman, Amelia. I love you, sweetheart."

CHAPTER TWENTY ONE
ETHAN

"S hit!" My thumb throbs instantly when it connects with the hammer.

"Sounds like the hammer won," Boone says, walking through the screen door with Ian behind him.

I shake out the pain. "What are you two doing here?"

"I've been trying to call you to tell you we have cattle to go look at in Tennessee."

"I turned the phone off." I pull it out of my back pocket.

"One of the city council members asked that I accompany you to the first session to help you get a good feel for the job."

"Fine by me. When do we leave?"

He glances at his watch. "Five minutes ago."

Ian takes the hammer from my grip. "I came to finish the repairs for your mother. Ellie said you'd been working here all morning trying to get them done for her."

"There's no time for discussion. Get in the truck. We'll stop by your place for a change of clothes," Boone grumbles.

"Damn, Ethan. Were you even watching where you were swinging this thing, or were you daydreaming?" Ian rubs his hand over the hole in the drywall.

"Construction is your area of expertise, not mine." I brush him off, not wanting to admit I was thinking about the last time I saw Jane with Matthew and pictured the nail was his face. Bad idea at the time. "Thanks for finishing the job for me. I'm sure she'll appreciate it." I follow Boone to the truck and climb inside. He drives to my place, and within minutes we're on the road headed to Tennessee.

"How is your mother liking Salt Lick?" Boone's gaze shifts from the road to me, then back on the road.

"I think she's adjusted far better than I ever thought she would."

"I believe Chet is enjoying having her around." He smiles.

"What?" I tilt my head in his direction.

"You'd have to be blind not to see it. He likes her."

"He isn't her type." I roll down the window letting the breeze cool my skin.

"Since when has that ever stopped two people from caring about each other." He chuckles.

"Great. My mother has a love life, and I'm destined to be alone."

"I take it that means things aren't going well between you and Jane?"

"Evidently, I'm the kind of man that plays second fiddle to others. First, Ellie with Ian, and now Jane with her old flame."

"Maybe you've misconstrued the situation. Noah's told me he hurt Jane badly with their breakup. Are you sure she's choosing Matthew over you?"

"I'm not giving her the chance. I ended it. Besides, I don't want her if she has feelings for another man. I want the woman that loves me to have no doubts. I've asked her to marry me two different times, and she said no to every one of my proposals."

"Seriously?" He stares at me.

"I'm done. I'm going to focus on my job and start building my own home. It's time. When I came here all those years ago, I had no intention of staying, but I fell in love with the life."

"My gut tells me you're wrong about Jane. I've seen the familiar way you two look at each other. It's the same between Clem and me."

"That's another thing I would never have believed when Clem made her way home. Never in a million years did she think you two would get back together. She'd say there was too much water under the bridge." I angle toward him. "She left you at the altar. How did you ever forgive her?"

"It wasn't easy. I blamed her for a lot of years. It wasn't until she came back that I realized it was just as much my fault as hers. She wasn't ready. Neither was I, but I was so in love with her, it didn't matter. Neither one of us dealt with losing the baby back then. I honestly feel if we'd have made it down the altar that day, it wouldn't have lasted. We both needed time to grow up and figure things out."

"She's the happiest I've ever seen her."

"We both are. Having Rose has only added to that." A smile covers his face talking about his two girls.

"You think you and Clem will ever have a child of your own?"

"Rose is as much ours as if Clem birthed her herself."

"She's lucky you found her."

"We're lucky. I'm not sure Clem will ever try to

get pregnant again. The two losses were awfully hard on her. On both of us." He lets his window down and rests his arm on it. "What about you? Do you want kids one day?"

"I don't know. Sometimes I think I do. I was lucky to have two good parents. You don't see that much anymore. Most kids are coming from broken homes. I had so many friends growing up that were tossed between their moms and dads. It screwed them up." I lower my hat over my eyes and lean back. "Wake me up when we get there."

❧

Dust fills my throat before I pull my bandanna over my nose. The dirt arena that normally houses a rodeo is being used to auction off cattle. The smell is a mixture of cow dung and hay. The stadium-style seating is filled with ranchers and the livestock agents representing them.

I lean on the metal railing to get a good look at the merchandise. "Whose brand is that?" I ask Boone, pointing to the brand on the hind end of one of the bulls.

"That beast is from the Murdock Brothers out of Montana. He's about a twelve-hundred pounder and sells for around sixty thousand dollars."

"Good thing we're not in need of a new steer."

"No, but two of our local ranchers are in need of a new one."

"Howdy, boys." A young woman dressed in blue jeans, boots, and a plaid shirt shimmies up next to Boone. "Who's your friend?" she asks, winking at me.

Boone stands tall, tucking his hands in his pockets. "This is Salt Lick's new livestock agent, Ethan York. Ethan, this is the only Murdock sister, Sierra."

She brushes by Boone. "It's so nice to meet you," she says, extending her hand.

"Nice to meet you, too."

"Where have you been hiding him all these years?" She elbows Boone in the gut.

"He ain't interested, Sierra. Keep your claws to yourself."

"That ain't no way to talk to a lady." She pouts.

"I'm here to work, not play." I try to blow her off nicely.

"Why don't you let me show you around." She loops her hand around my arm and drags me away from Boone. I glance back over my shoulder, and he shrugs.

"I have the inside scoop on all things cattle."

She rattles on for the next hour, and surprisingly, I learn a lot from her. She says she's been doing this since she was knee-high to a grasshopper. By the way she talks, I believe it.

"Buy me a drink." She motions toward a concession stand.

I pull out my wallet. "What would you like?"

"Whatever cold beer they are selling." She climbs the railing overlooking the arena and sits on the top metal slate.

After I purchase two beers, I join her.

"I don't see a ring on your finger," she says, grabbing the amber bottle from me.

"Nope," I respond, taking a sip.

"You spoken for?" She runs her fingers through the hair by my ear.

I inhale deeply and take a good long look at her. She's pretty with her long rose-colored hair. Her eyes are as green as the grass in the fields, and she's got curves in all the right places to boot. She's shorter and a tad bit heavier than Jane but equally as pretty. "If you're asking me if I'm taken, the answer is yes."

"Too bad. You and I could have some fun together."

"The auction prices are being posted." A heavy hand rests on my back. I turn to see Boone. "You need to review them."

I hop down. "Thank you for showing me the ropes." I tilt my hat at Sierra.

"Anytime, cowboy. The offer still stands if you change your mind," she hollers as we walk away.

"I thought you and Jane were done," Boone states.

"We are."

"Not what I overheard." He laughs.

"Can we just focus on the job at hand? No more talk of Jane." I stomp past him as if I know where I'm going.

"Hey!" he yells.

I glare over my shoulder. "It's this way." He points, a shit-eating grin on his face.

I follow him, and we study the boards. He draws attention to a few numbers and names of buyers who generally sell for good prices. Then he introduces me to them.

We all end up sitting around one of the rectangle tables, negotiating deals while downing bottles of beer. My mind drifts to the night I got drunk and showed up at Jane's. I'm an idiot. It's obvious why she chose her old boyfriend over me.

Sierra takes a seat beside her brothers. Her stare is glued to me. It would be so easy to give in to her. One-night stands used to be my thing in the military. No commitments. Half the time, I didn't even learn their names. *Damn it*. I can't do it. I've spent the last year prancing around the woman I love. I tried really hard to stay away from her. She was off-limits. Too bad my heart didn't listen to my head.

Boone stands, bringing my thoughts back to the here and now. "Thank you, gentlemen."

Sierra clears her throat.

"And Sierra." He nods in her direction. "I believe we have everything we need." He casts a look at me.

"Yes, thank you." I position myself next to him. We all shake hands before we leave, and I feel Sierra slip something into my hand.

"In case you decide your cowgirl ain't enough for you."

I give her the piece of paper back, and she shoves it in my pocket.

We exit the arena and start the drive into town to find a hotel for the night. Once we get checked in, we head to the local steak house.

We order our food and drinks. The jukebox is lit up and playing a Willie Nelson song.

"What is it women want?" I lean on the table closer to Boone so he can hear me over the music.

"Hell, if I know," he snorts.

"You must. You seem to keep Clem happy."

"They want a man they can trust, and that will protect them at all costs. They want you not only to tell them every day you love them, but they want you to show them too. At least that's what Clem says." He inches closer. "Sex works, too, and lots of it."

"Sex isn't our problem."

He picks up a bottle of beer and downs it, setting it hard on the table when he's done. "Then you need to figure out what the real issue is before you completely call it quits."

"I've already ended it."

He chuckles. "If that were true, Sierra would have you in one of those hotel rooms right now. Not too many men resist her charms."

"Have you..."

"Hell no. I don't like easy women. Besides, I have my hands full with Clem." He smiles.

"I don't know. Things are much simpler without a woman in my life."

"Yeah, but they ain't near as fun."

CHAPTER TWENTY TWO
JANE

"Ethan!" I holler as my feet hit the porch step. I swing open the door without banging on it and nearly knock Ian off a ladder.

"Whoa!" he says, trying to keep his balance.

"Sorry. Is Ethan here?"

"You just missed him. He and Boone took off for Tennessee. They had cattle to assess."

"Oh." I bite my bottom lip. "Do you know when they'll be back?"

"They didn't say."

"How did you get roped into doing the repairs?" I stare up at him.

"I like this sort of thing. Besides, I needed a break from Ellie and the baby."

"I'll be sure not to tell her that." I giggle.

"Deacon is teething, and he's been up all night. Ellie is akin to Betty White without a Snickers bar when she's tired." He chuckles. "I'm safer out of the house."

"You and Ellie are happy, right?" I hold on to the ladder.

"Yes." He points the paintbrush tipped in yellow at me. "What's wrong? You and Ethan at odds?"

"He saw me and Matthew together and got the wrong impression.'"

"Ah," he says.

"What's that supposed to mean?" I scowl.

He climbs down the ladder, placing the paintbrush on the can. "Ethan ain't one to play seconds. Especially after Ellie. And, I can't say I blame him. He's been dancing around his feelings for you for a while. He was cautious, and he finally made his move, then Matthew came to town. I'm sure it reminded him of the situation with me and Ellie."

"You love Ellie, and the two of you were meant to be together. I don't love Matthew. Hell, I don't even like him."

"I'm not the one that needs convincing."

I dial Ethan's cell from the phone that's been gripped in my hand. "He won't answer. How am I supposed to get it through his thick head if he won't talk to me?"

"He eventually has to come home. I'd take up camp in his cabin if I were you."

"That's a great idea. Thanks, Ian. Tell Ellie if she needs a break, to bring Deacon to Magnolia Mill. He can play with his cousins."

"I'm sure she'll take you up on it." I open the door to leave. "Jane." Ian says my name. "Good luck."

I nod, leaving with more determination to convince Ethan how I feel about him. It was such a nice day that I walked to Ethan's mom's house, leaving my car at the main house. I take the dirt road, heading to Ethan's. I try his phone again, and he still doesn't answer. When I round the corner by Ellie's house to Ethan's small cabin, I see the rental car Matthew's been driving around town.

"What the hell are you doing here?" I beat on the driver's side window.

He opens the door, hopping out. "I was looking for Ethan."

"How did you know where he lives?" I press my finger against his chest.

"I asked around town. He's pretty popular with the women here."

"I told you to leave town." I cross my arms over my chest.

"The man you claim to love needs to know the truth, and if you ain't gonna tell him, I am."

I dial Noah's number. "We have an intruder on the property. Come to Ethan's place and bring a gun," I say before Matthew snatches it out of my hand. He tosses it on the ground, pressing the heel of his boot on it until the screen crunches beneath it.

"It ain't gonna matter. Noah will be here and put a bullet in your ass!" I'm inches from his face.

He quickly jerks my arm, wrenching it behind my back. "You'll be long gone before he arrives." He pushes me with his body to the trunk of his car.

"Let go of me!" He twists harder as I try to free myself from his grasp.

Popping the trunk open, he grabs something out of it. I stomp hard on his foot, but he doesn't let go. He covers my mouth with a white cloth, and an obnoxious scent fills my mouth and nose. A wave of nausea hits me before my sight blurs. My body goes limp. Matthew catches me before I hit the ground and places me gently in the trunk of his car. The lights grow dimmer when he closes me inside.

I HEAR A BUMPING SOUND AS I FIGHT TO OPEN MY eyes. It's pitch-black other than a hint of a brake light seeping through the trunk. The taste in my mouth has my stomach retching. I roll to the side, but nothing but drool comes out, moistening my dry mouth, enabling me to scream.

"Let me out!" I beat my fist on the trunk lid.

My body jerks as he hits the brakes. I hear the car door open and boots hitting the pavement. "I'm not letting you out until I get to where we're going, so you might as well save your energy," I hear him say.

"Noah is going to find you and kill you for this!" My fist makes contact with the metal.

"We'll be long gone before he can find you."

"Where are you taking me?" I scream.

"Home."

Another wave rolls through my gut. "Please don't do this."

"You forced my hand. This is all your fault. If you'd have just come peacefully, none of this would be happening."

I have to keep my wits about me. What would make him let me out of here so I can get free of him? "I'm sorry. You're right. You and I belong together." He's so quiet I think he's gone. "Matthew? You still out there?"

"I want to believe you." I hear the doubt in his voice.

"I'll prove it to you. Let me out of here, and I promise you won't regret it." I cross my fingers behind my back like I used to when I was a little girl telling a lie.

"You promise to come with me peacefully?"

"Yes." I swallow my lie. If I know where I am, I'll run as fast as I can.

With the press of a button, the trunk opens. I shield my eyes, fully expecting the daylight to blind me, but it doesn't. It's dusk. How long have we been on the road?

"You promised you wouldn't run." He holds his hand out to me, helping me out. I look around, but I'm clueless as to where we are. "Get in the car," he orders.

I walk around to the passenger side, sliding inside. He gets behind the wheel and starts the car moving. I'm silent, watching for anything I might recognize. We're on a long, winding road with no street signs. Vehicles are sparse on the road.

"Where are we going?"

"We'll drive a few more miles then find a motel for the night. Since you've agreed to come with me, we'll catch a plane tomorrow back to Texas."

Good. Once we're in a crowd, I'll be able to get away from him if there's no escaping him tonight. He's utterly lost his mind if he thinks I'm flying home with him. "I need to use your cell phone to call Noah. He'll come looking for me if I don't call him off." I hold my hand out.

"I don't trust you."

"You know he knows where you live. He'll hunt you down."

"Fine. You have one minute." He hands it to me.

I dial in Noah's number.

"Where the fuck are you?" His voice blares through the speaker.

"I decided to go back to Texas with Matthew. Please don't follow us."

He shouts several curse words.

"Look, I know you're angry, and I know you know how much I hate to fly, but it'll all be okay. Just like when we were kids, I'll recite my mantra. You remember it, right?" I don't let him respond. "I will fly like the *red* bird in the sky." Noah will understand. He knows red is my word for when I'm in real trouble. "Tell Ethan I'm sorry." I motion as if I hang up but leave the line open. "There, are you happy?"

"You did sound awful convincing." He takes his eyes off the road to look at me.

"How much longer before we stop? I have to pee."

We round a corner, and he points to a road sign. "Five miles to Fern Creek," he says.

"Fern Creek," I repeat, then slide my hand over

his phone, ending the call with Noah. I hand it back to him.

"After we get a room, I'll take you to dinner. We can celebrate."

I plaster on a fake smile. "I'd like that."

Five miles later, we're pulling into the small town of Fern Creek. He parks outside a wooden lodge that has a trail of rooms attached to it.

"I'll wait in the car while you check us in," I say.

I think he's going to leave me until he shuts his door, marching to my side and opening the car. "I want to trust you, but I'm not sold yet." He holds it open. "Don't even think about running." He taps his jacket pocket with a warning.

He has a gun? He wouldn't shoot me, would he? Noah will find me. Then he grabs my arm, digging his fingers in so hard I'll have a bruise. I attempt to yank free, but he jerks me even harder.

"Stop! You're going to make me hurt you," he snarls.

"When did you start abusing women?"

"I guess we've both changed to get the things we want."

"How have I changed?"

"You're mouthy. You used to be sweet." He stops walking. "Keep your mouth shut while I check us in. If you don't, you won't be the only one I'll hurt."

He's sick. I wasn't afraid of him until right this minute. I purse my lips together and nod. I need to keep my cool and wait for Noah. He holds the door open for me to step inside.

"We need a room for the night," he says to the gray-haired man behind the counter.

"You two are in luck. We have one room left," he says, handing him papers to fill out.

He's making it real easy for Noah to find us by signing his real name. Amateur move.

"Do I know you," the man asks.

"I don't believe so," I respond.

He snaps his fingers. "I've seen your picture in the paper. You're the mayor of Salt Lick."

"You're mistaken," Matt says gruffly, giving him the paperwork back. "My wife is from Texas."

I look down, biting my lip.

He hands Matt the keys, and he takes my hand in his to walk out. As he opens the door, I glance over my shoulder and give the man a slight nod.

"Looks like we are the last room on the end." He keeps me glued to his side as he unlocks the room. "Are you hungry?"

"I'm still nauseous from whatever you drugged me with." I walk inside, turning on the light. There is one double bed in the middle of the dingy room. "Not your typical place to stay for the night."

"The nausea will subside." He tosses the keys on the dresser. "The room will have to do."

"You're sleeping on the floor." I sit on the edge of the brown bedspread.

"Like hell I am." He glares at me.

"What makes you think as soon as your eyes close, I'm not running as far from you as I can?"

"I won't be sleeping," he says, stepping in front of me. "I'm not taking my eyes off of you until we're home."

"Do you plan on locking me in the attic?"

He squats and tucks a strand of hair behind my ear. "Why can't you just remember how much you love me?"

"Loved. Past tense."

"You'll change your mind."

"I won't. As a matter of fact, don't be so sure I won't kill you in your sleep."

He stands, taking the revolver out of this jacket pocket. "Then I guess this will come in handy after all."

"I don't remember you owning a gun." I swallow hard.

"I had a feeling you wouldn't come willingly." He sits in the small chair and crosses one leg over the other with his gun in his lap.

"Why would you want a woman who doesn't want you? What's happened to you?"

He juts his chin in the air. "You happened to me."

"You threw me out like a piece of trash!"

"I can admit my mistakes, but when are you going to admit that you are partially to blame?"

"How do you figure?"

"You were young and had no idea how to meet a man's needs. It didn't matter to me at the time because you were so damn beautiful."

I laugh. "You think you were my Prince Charming? You were a selfish lover."

"I never heard you complain."

"That's because you didn't listen."

He places his feet on the ground and leans on his knees, remaining in the chair. "I'm listening now."

"You are unfucking real! You haven't paid any attention to anything I've told you. I. Don't. Love. You."

"Once we get home, you will. I'll give you anything and everything you need. You'll want for nothing."

"Is that so?" I walk toward him. "What happens if I get sick again?"

"You won't."

"I can reject my kidney at any time."

"If and when that happens, I'll deal with it."

"How? You made it very clear you didn't want a broken woman. Someone you had to take care of." I pace the floor in front of him. "Even if I could go back and forgive you for the things you said, I'd never forgive you for sleeping with another woman."

"You'll be in my bed every night. There will be no need for anyone else."

"You've lost your mind!" I throw my hands in the air. "I will never sleep with you again!"

He places the gun back in his pocket and stands, grabbing my hips and pulling me flush with him. "You will, given time."

I turn my face away from him when he tries to kiss me. He grips my face hard and presses his lips to mine. I open slightly and bite him hard. He draws back, and there's blood on his bottom lip. He rears back, slapping me across the face.

I gasp, rubbing my cheek.

"You need to be tamed," he says, wiping the blood from his lip.

This is not the same man I left in Texas. He had his faults, but he never laid a hand on me, much less threaten me with a gun. I can't wait for Noah to rescue me. I have to get away from him. I rush toward the door, and he snatches me around the waist and tosses me on the bed.

He balls his hand into a fist. "I'm going to teach you a lesson."

The door crashes open, and Noah charges toward him, knocking Matt to the ground.

CHAPTER TWENTY THREE
BEAR

"Hey, sugar," I say as Nita and I walk into Missy's bedroom.

She looks up from the book she's reading. "Am I in trouble?" She pouts.

"What makes you think you're in trouble?" I sit on the edge of her bed and run my hand over her hair.

"Usually, when the two of you come in here together, I'm getting a lecture for something I did wrong." She suddenly sits straight up. "Did something happen to Momma Sandy?"

"No. She's where she needs to be in rehab. I do think we need to send you back to counseling again."

"You've been through a lot. We only want to make sure you're okay," Nita tells her.

Missy squints her eyes. "That's not the reason you two are here."

I grab Nita's hand and sit her on my lap. "No, it's not."

Missy plops back. "Please don't tell me any bad news."

"I think you're going to like what we want to share with you."

"Am I getting my own horse?" Her eyes light up.

"Something even better."

"What's better than a horse?" She rolls her eyes.

I place my hand on Nita's belly. "We're having a baby."

Missy squeals as she stands on the bed, jumping up and down. "Yay! A baby sister!"

"Or a baby brother." I tug her hand, and she joins Nita on my lap.

"That is better than a horse." She hugs Nita's neck. "Thank you so much."

"I'm glad you're happy, sweetheart."

"Can I call Rose and tell her?"

"We are all going over to Grandpa's house to tell the family together. Go get your shoes on." She hops off my lap.

"Are you sure you're ready for the entire clan to know you're expecting?"

"Are you worried?" Nita softly places her hand on

my cheek.

"If I'm being completely honest, I'm concerned about me being a father again. I love Missy with my entire being, but it was hard being a single dad. I could've never done it without the support of my family."

"You're not alone this time. I will never leave you or our children." She kisses me sweetly.

"I do worry about Clem every time a Calhoun announces having a baby."

"Clem will be so excited for us, and Missy."

"I know, but it has to tear at her heart."

"You are such a good husband, father, and brother. The luckiest day of my life was the day you caught me stealing that car."

"I promise you I will always put our marriage first. I can't promise we won't go through hard times, but I will love you no matter what, and our children."

"I have no doubt you will, and I promise the same."

"Daddy. Where do babies come from anyway?" Missy bounces back into the room.

"That's a discussion for another day. Nita will explain it to you," I say as we both stand.

Nita slaps me in the gut. "Thanks a lot."

"If this one's a boy, it will be my job."

"Do I get to name the baby?" Missy asks, slipping

her hand into Nita's as we head to the main house.

"Do you have something specific in mind?"

"If it's a boy, I like Walker."

"Walker Calhoun. That's a good name." I tug her ponytail. "What if it's a girl?"

"Elsa, of course." She rolls her eyes again, and we both laugh. She skips out ahead of us, and I wrap my arm around Nita's waist.

"Maybe Elsa could be the middle name." She grins.

"The naming thing is all yours. I got to name Missy, but I do like Walker."

"How about Bradley Walker Calhoun?" She looks up at me.

"I'd say I'm hoping for a son."

Missy moves back in our direction. "Do I get to tell everyone?"

"I think we should let Momma Nita."

"I've been meaning to ask you something?" She gazes up at Nita.

"You can ask me anything."

"Now that Momma Sandy won't be around anymore, can I just call you momma?"

"I would love that." Nita hugs her neck. I see Nita wipe away a tear. Missy runs up the porch steps into the house.

"Thank you for giving me such a sweet daughter."

"I'm thankful you love her so much." I lead her into the house.

Dad is sitting at the table with Winnie. Clem and Boone are filling glasses with ice. Ellie, Ian, and Deacon are chatting with Wyatt and Margret while the twins sit on her lap. Rose is already huddled in the corner with Missy.

"What's this meeting all about? We have someone after our land again?" Daddy asks.

"No, nothing like that. We're still missing a few people. Where's Jane, Noah, Ethan, and Molly?"

"Sorry I'm late," Ethan says, coming through the back door as Molly walks through the front door without Noah.

"Where's Noah?"

"I don't know. I've been trying to call him, but it goes straight to voicemail."

"What about Jane?" I turn my question to Ethan.

"I don't know. I haven't spoken to her."

"Whatever you're wanting to tell us, we can fill them in when they show up," Chet says.

I take Nita's hand in mine. "He's right. Go ahead and tell them the news."

The room is dead quiet. Nita clears her throat. "Bear and I are having a baby."

"Oh my gawd. That's fantastic." Clem is the first to hug her.

"This family is growing by leaps and bounds." Ellie kisses her cheek.

"I could use another grandson." Chet chuckles.

Winnie reaches over, patting his hand. "I think whether it's a boy or a girl, you're going to spoil them rotten."

"That's the pot calling the kettle black. I saw the shipment of toys and clothes you purchased for all the kiddos."

"Guilty." She giggles. "Since my son doesn't seem to be in a hurry to make me a grandmother, I'll consider this as mine like all the Calhouns.'"

"I'm so happy for the two of you." Margret gets in on hugging Nita too.

Ian, Boone, Wyatt, and Ethan shake my hand.

"Congratulations, man." Boone slaps me on the back.

"Thanks. I couldn't be happier."

"You and Noah are next," Ian tells Ethan.

"I'll leave that up to Noah and Molly. It's not in the cards for me," Ethan responds, a sad look in his eyes. "I have been meaning to talk to you about building my house. I'm ready whenever you have time to start."

"I can have it going within the month." Ian walks with Ethan to the living room to discuss details.

"Where is Jane?" I ask Molly.

"I just tried her phone, and it goes to voicemail too." Her phone rings as she's holding it in her hand. "Hey, babe. Where are you?" She scowls and covers her mouth with her hand. "Did you find her?" Her voice cracks, and we all stop what we're doing and listen to her end of the conversation. "Did you call the police?"

"What the hell is going on?" Chet stands.

Molly holds up her hand. "Call me as soon as you find her."

"What happened to Jane?" Ethan's voice is filled with concern.

"I'm not sure. Noah got a call from Matt's number. It was Jane. He said she used her safe word the two of them created when they were younger. He heard where Matt was headed before he got disconnected."

"What the hell is she doing with Matt?" Wyatt asks.

"They were getting back together," Ethan answers.

"Bullshit." Chet slams his fist on the table.

"Noah was trying to track Jane's phone, but he says there's no signal." Molly paces the floor.

Ethan takes out his phone and dials her number. "He's right. Nothing. Where did he say he was headed?"

"Fern Creek."

"That's only thirty minutes from here." I look at my watch. "We should get on the road."

"Noah said to tell everyone to stay put, and he'd call us when he finds her."

"I can't sit here and do nothing." Ethan storms out the door.

"I'm so sorry, Bear and Nita. I didn't mean to ruin your day," Molly says.

"It's not your fault."

"I should have seen something like this happening." Wyatt runs his hand through his hair. "He's been stalking after Jane since he stepped foot in town."

"I think we need to go after her." Chet takes one of his rifles off the wall.

"We need to trust Noah. He's already on their tails. By the time we get to her, Noah will already have the situation handled," Boone states.

"What do you mean by handled?" Molly asks.

"He'll do whatever needs to be done," Daddy barks.

Clem walks to Molly's side. "This is the hardest part about this family. We fight hard, and we love hard. We protect one another at all costs. It was a lesson not easily learned by me. It almost cost me my marriage. Noah will not let anything happen to Jane."

"Who's going to make sure nothing happens to Noah?" Tears fill her eyes.

Ellie joins them. "Noah and Jane have a strong bond, and they've always taken care of each other."

Ethan's boots rattle the wood floor when the door flies open. "Are any of you coming with me?" He has Daddy's shotgun in tow.

This is a side of Ethan I've never seen. He's always the calm one.

"Ethan York! You put that thing down and get your head on straight. All you're going to do is get yourself killed or someone else." Winnie's words are stern as she presses a finger against his shoulder. "I know you love her. I have faith Noah will bring her home safely."

"You have no idea how things are done around here, Mother."

"In this instance, she's right." Boone walks toward him, taking the shotgun from his grip. "You'd be chasing your tail trying to find her without Noah."

Ethan grinds his jaw. "What if it were Clem? Would you sit around and wait, hoping he'd find her, or would you march out the door with pistols blaring?"

Boone breathes out heavily. "I'd go after her."

Ethan holds up his phone. "I've tracked Noah's location."

CHAPTER TWENTY FOUR
JANE

"Noah! He has a gun!" I warn him as they grapple on the floor.

Matt's nose crunches underneath the pounding of Noah's fist. He wails out in pain as blood spews down his nose. His hand flies to his face as the other hand draws the gun from his coat pocket.

Noah jumps off him, holding his hands in the air. I rush to stand in front of him. "No!" I scream.

Matt manages to get to his feet. "Get the hell out of here, Noah!" He aims at me. "I'll kill her if you don't."

"Put the gun down," Noah says, calmly. "You don't want to hurt her."

His aim adjusts to Noah. "Then I'll take you out instead. You were always a pain in my ass, trying to convince Jane to leave me. It's your fault she left Texas."

"I made my own decision. Noah had nothing to do with me leaving you." I step closer to him. "Let him go, and I'll go back to Texas with you without a fight."

His gaze bounces back and forth between Noah and me. "I don't believe you."

"I give you my word."

"No. You can't go with him!" Noah barks, bumping into the back of me.

Both of Matt's hands grip the gun tighter. "Leave, now!"

I turn around, and I'm face to face with Noah. "I'll be okay. He's not going to hurt me."

"He already has. Look at your face. It would've been ten times worse had I not found you when I did."

"Enough chitchat!" I glance over my shoulder to see Matt's finger on the trigger. "You have five seconds to get out of there before I start shooting. Don't even think about following us."

"Please go. I have no doubt he'll kill you."

Noah's jaw flexes back and forth. "This isn't over!"

"It better be, or I'll end her life."

"Please, Noah, I'm begging you. You have a family to think about."

"You are my family."

"Molly needs you. I'll do as he asks, and I'll be fine. Now go." I know every ounce of Noah doesn't want to walk out that door and leave me with Matthew. In my heart, I know he'll find a way to rescue me.

He begrudgingly opens the door. "If you kill her, I'll leave no stone unturned to hunt you down, and I will show no mercy."

I see a glint of fear in Matthew's eyes. "As long as she keeps her promise not to fight me, she'll be unharmed."

Noah closes the door behind him, and Matt walks over to the window, pushing aside the curtain to watch him get in his truck. His gun is trained on me. "As soon as he drives away, we're getting out of here. We have a long drive ahead of us."

"I thought we were catching a plane."

"Plans changed the minute your brother showed up."

"I don't understand why you're doing this."

"I've already told you. I love you."

"This isn't love. It's possession."

"Call it what you will, but you will be my wife."

"You need help."

"He's gone." He holds open the door. "Get in my car."

"Can you quit waving the gun in my face? I've already told you I'd go willingly."

"I don't trust you for one minute."

"What a great way to start a marriage," I say sarcastically, opening the passenger side door.

"Just get in the car."

He shuts it and walks around the other side while keeping his gun targeted on me through the window.

I hit the lock button, and he almost jerks the handle off trying to open it.

"Unlock it now!" he screams, and I ignore him.

The butt of his gun smacks against the window, sending shards of glassing flying inside. A piece rips through the skin under my left eye. I press the heel of my hand against it to keep it from bleeding.

He yanks my hand down to look at it. "It will serve as a reminder to you to not fuck with me."

He places the gun in his lap and buckles up before he starts the car. At some point, he'll let his guard down, and I'll shoot him with it.

I watch out the side mirror to see if Noah's headlights fall in behind us. Nothing but darkness follows. I know he's out there somewhere. He'd never let Matthew win.

"Why don't you try to get some rest. It's going to be a long night."

"Like I could sleep," I say, leaning my head against

the window. His demeanor seems to relax a bit as we ride in silence.

"What do you really expect to get out of this? A happily ever after from a woman you've kidnapped."

"One day, you'll thank me for rescuing you from this shithole town."

I straighten my spine. "I love my life in Salt Lick."

He mimics my words from earlier. "Loved. Past tense."

"I love my family and my work."

"How could you possibly love your father? He deserted you and your brother."

"I was wrong about what happened between him and my mother. He's a good man, and he saved my life without question." I turn to face him. "You, on the other hand, would not bother getting tested to see if you were a match. Not the act of a man who claims to love me."

"I wasn't going to let them nearly cut me in half to save you," he snarls.

"A man that truly loved me would have." I cross my arms over my chest.

"I thought you were going to die. If you loved me, you wouldn't have asked me to risk my life for yours."

"I never asked you for anything. In fact, I never asked my family, but every one of them stood in line to be tested without even knowing me. That's love. You're just a narcissistic asshole."

"And you need your mouth washed out with soap." He scowls at me.

"Oh"—I laugh—"this coming from the man who, not ten minutes ago, held a gun to my head, threatening to kill me."

"You have changed. You would've never spoken this way to me before."

"I've grown a pair of balls, thanks to you."

"Once we are married, you won't speak that way to me anymore." He points at me.

"I said I'd leave peacefully with you. I don't recall agreeing to marry you."

"You will marry me, or I'll hire someone to wreak havoc on that so-called family of yours you love so much."

"You wouldn't dare!" I glare.

"Try me. You'll marry me at the justice of the peace as soon as we get back, or I'll follow through on my promise."

"Ha! Don't you want a big wedding to show me off?"

"I do, but I know you'd never agree to it."

"Like I'd agree to a justice of the peace shotgun wedding either. What is it you really want?"

"A beautiful woman by my side. Someone who will make me look good to the right people."

"What's the matter? Have you lost your touch? Maybe people have seen right through your facade. You used to be such a smooth talker," I snicker.

"You don't know what you're talking about." He growls, gripping the wheel tighter.

"Did your four-inch dick get caught doing the naughty with one of your bosses' wives?"

I place my hand on the dash, waiting for the abrupt stop to slam me forward.

"You bitch!" he seethes, standing on the brake. The car screeches across the pavement. His body jerks, and I take the split second of time I have to reach over and grab his gun before it falls on the floorboard.

His forehead bounces off the steering wheel, causing his nose to start bleeding again. Searching his lap for the gun, he comes up empty-handed, and his bloody face turns in my direction.

I have the gun held tightly in my hand. "How does it feel having this cold piece of metal aimed directly at you?"

"You won't shoot me."

"Are you willing to bet your life on it?" I place my index finger lightly on the trigger. "Turn this car around and head back to town." We're out in the middle of nowhere in complete darkness other than the headlights of the car.

"You made a promise to come with me in exchange for your brother's life."

"I changed my mind."

"I will have him killed."

"That's kinda hard to do if you're dead."

"I know you, Jane. You can't kill a fly."

He's right. I act all big and brave, but it's not in me to kill another human being. As much as I want him dead, I can't pull the trigger. "Get out of the car." I gnash my teeth.

"What?"

"You heard me, get out of the car."

Fragments of glass crunch as he opens the door, getting out.

I open mine, meeting him on the other side with my hand held out. "I saw you take the keys. Give them to me."

"Look, we can still work this out without either one of us getting hurt. I love you, Jane."

Is he serious? I think he's lost his ever-loving mind. "Just give me the keys."

He takes them out of his pocket and dangles them above my hand. "If you want them, you'll have to find them." He rears back with his arm and throws them into the dark woods.

"Son of a bitch!" I press the gun to his head.

"You aren't going to shoot me, Jane." He places his hand on the gun and lowers it. "You may have changed, but not that much."

I tuck the gun in the back of my slacks and start walking in the direction we came from.

He comes up from behind me, tackling me to the ground. My face hits hard, and I feel the laceration below my eye start to bleed. He straddles me, pressing my cheek to the asphalt and takes his weapon back.

I hear the sound of a diesel engine barreling down the road before I see its light turn on, blinding me. Matthew snatches me by the hair to bring me to my feet.

The truck slams to a stop, and multiple feet hit the ground. Blinking a few times to clear my vision, I recognize Wyatt's truck.

"Let her go!" Ethan's voice blares out from the dark.

The gun drills into my side, and he wraps his arm around my throat.

"Get back, or I'll shoot her," Matt snarls.

"You're outnumbered." Boone is to the side of us, aiming a rifle.

"That might be, but you'll have to shoot her to get to me."

"Please stop. Nobody has to die here tonight," I cry out. "Let me go before it's too late," I plead.

"I should've run your ass out of town the first minute I laid eyes on you." Wyatt is on the other side with a rifle burrowed into his shoulder.

"The police are on their way," Bear says, standing next to Boone.

Noah joins them. "I told you this wasn't over."

"Give me the keys to your truck." He wrenches my head back.

"That's not going to happen." Ethan's roar is menacing. "You aren't leaving here with her."

"I said, give me your keys!" He shoves the gun into my temple, and I wince.

Wyatt drops his weapon to his side. "I'll give them to you if you let her go."

"Not happening. This is going to play out my way or else."

I hear the sirens and see the swirl of blue lights coming quickly down the road.

"You hear that sound? You have until the count of three. They can either be arresting you or placing a white chalk line around your dead body. Your choice," Noah barks.

"Get the hell out of my way." He snatches the keys from Wyatt's hand and walks backward with his arm still around my throat to the truck.

It's now or never. I don't want my family to kill him.

"One," Noah starts the count.

"Two," Ethan snaps.

I lean my head forward, and with all my might, slam it into Matt's nose. He releases me as he falls against the trunk, and I go to the ground.

Ethan rushes to my side, and Noah jerks the gun from Matthew's grip.

"Please don't kill him," I cry.

Ethan's scowled brow and darkened eyes look as if I shoved a knife in his gut.

Boone turns Matthew facing the truck and pins him against it. The police pull up just in time. Boone shoves him forcefully in their direction. Noah stands with the officers, telling them what happened. I watch as Matthew is cuffed.

"We need to get you to the hospital." Ethan helps me off the ground.

"I'm fine."

He walks me in front of the headlights and tilts my chin up. "You need stitches."

Suddenly, I feel woozy and light-headed. My knees buckle, and Ethan scoops me into his arms. I faintly hear one of the officers asking him if we need an ambulance.

"No," he answers, laying me in the back seat of the truck. "I'll take her myself."

"We'll need her for questioning," an officer states.

"When I know she's okay, she'll answer all your questions." Ethan slides in beside me, protectively tucking me into his side. After Matthew is in the back seat of the police car, they cram into the truck. Ethan eases me into his lap for more room.

I feel the trickle of warm blood running down my face. Ethan moves me forward as he peels out of his shirt. "This will stop the bleeding." He holds it to my face, and I rest against Ethan's chest, suddenly feeling exhausted.

"Thank you," I whisper and doze off to sleep.

It seems like only seconds later, he's waking me up at the emergency room doors of the hospital. "Is this really necessary?" I mutter.

"I want the doctors to check you out. You look pretty beat-up." Ethan helps me out of the truck.

The waiting room is empty, and a nurse takes me right back. Within thirty minutes, a doctor examines me.

"I'd like to keep her overnight for observations. You've got a good-size lump on the back of your head."

"I want to go home." I gaze up at Ethan.

"You should stay."

His words find me empty. The look of heartache is back in his eyes. Does he think because I pleaded for Matt's life that I still have feelings for him? Now is not the time to make him see differently.

"I'll stay if you discharge me first thing in the morning," I tell the doctor.

"I'm not making any promises. I'll want to make sure all your tests come out okay."

"Don't worry, she's not going anywhere." Boone bursts through the curtain dividing the rooms.

"Fine." I roll my eyes, laying my head on the pillow, feeling defeated.

Ethan walks to the end of my bed. "Get some rest."

"Aren't you staying with me?"

He tucks his hands in his pocket, looking downward. "No," he answers simply.

The doctor steps up to me. "Visitors can't stay the night unless you're in the ICU. Hospital policy," he says.

Wyatt comes from behind the curtain. "I'm staying with her." He glares at the doctor.

He raises his hands in surrender. "You'll get a bed soon, Miss Calhoun." He leaves me surrounded by the men in my family.

"Wyatt. You don't have to stay. You have Margret and the twins to get home to."

"They'll be fine one night without me." He takes a seat in the metal chair beside the bed.

One by one, except for Ethan, they kiss my cheek, telling me bye. Ethan slipped out before I realized he was gone.

CHAPTER TWENTY FIVE
ETHAN

"So this is where you've been hiding." My mother bursts through my office door.

"This is called working, not hiding." I shut my laptop.

She nonchalantly walks through the door and takes a seat across from my desk. "Jane's been out of the hospital for three days, and you haven't seen her yet."

"I've been busy."

"Poor girl looks awful with the bruising on her face. I can only imagine what her heart looks like, all broken inside."

I clasp my hands together on the desk. "Is there a point to this conversation?"

"Wyatt brought her home, and he says she's done nothing but cry."

"And you think I'm responsible for her tears?"

"Boone told us what happened."

"Mother, I can't do this with you right now. I have work to do." I lean back in my chair.

"She loves you." She gives me that "I'm your mother, and I know best" look.

"And I love her, but I'm not going to be the second man in her heart. I choose to give her up."

"Oh, so what she wants doesn't really matter."

"You weren't there. I saw the look in her eyes as she pleaded for us not to kill the man who kidnapped her and beat her."

"You think she did that because she still loves him?" Her eyebrows raise.

"What other reason could there be?"

She slowly gets up, straightens her dress and walks over to my side of the desk, then pops me on the top of the head with her hand like she used to do when I was a child getting into trouble.

"What was that for?"

"I raised a smart man, and you're being an idiot."

"You're siding with her against your own son?"

"No. I'm knocking some sense into that thick skull of yours. Jane showed mercy on another human being, and it had nothing to do with her feelings for you," she scolds.

I blow out a long, hard breath. "Please stay out of it."

She lifts my chin to look at her. "You're my son, and you're hurting."

"You can't kiss it and make it all better, Mother. I'm not six years old."

"Then quit acting like a pouting child. Go talk to her."

I stand, kissing her forehead. "I love you, Mom, but I'm a grown man and can handle my own affairs."

Tears well up in her eyes. "I only want to see you happy."

"And I appreciate it."

She heads to my office door and turns to look at me with her finger pointed in my direction. "That girl loves you," she says, then walks out.

I spend the next two hours hidden in my office, trying to get work done, but my thoughts fall back on Jane. It took everything I had to leave her at the hospital. I wanted to stay by her side, but I couldn't stomach the thought of her still loving a man like Matthew.

I fumble through a few more phone calls and files before I call it quits. Gathering my things, I shut my door, heading to my truck. I stop by Ian's office to approve the plans for my house.

"You work quick." I shake his hand.

"You and I had already discussed what you wanted, so it was easy. We can have it completed in six months along with the mother-in-law suite."

"Thanks, man."

He stares at me for a moment. "You alright?"

"Yeah."

"You don't appear to be. I've seen that look before."

"What look?"

"The man with the broken heart because he didn't get the woman of his dreams." He chuckles.

"This is the second lecture I've gotten today. My mother stopped by my office to give me an earful."

"No lecture, only an observation."

"Thanks for your concern." I turn to leave.

"Don't lose a good thing because your feelings got hurt. Jane did the best she could in a terrifying situation. Matt's paying the price behind bars. That's a better revenge than him lying six feet under."

I nod, knowing he's right. Driving through town, I have every intention of going home, but my truck has a mind of its own when it does an illegal U-turn in the middle of town. Blue lights pop in behind me.

I pull over and see Mike getting out of his police car. I let the window down, and he leans on it. "You in a hurry to go somewhere?" He lowers his sunglasses to the bridge of his nose.

"Sorry. I wasn't thinking."

"Jane ain't in there with you, is she?" He pokes his head in and glances in the back seat.

"No."

"The U-turn you made back there is something she would do. That woman has a lead foot. You Calhouns keep me busy."

"I'm not a Calhoun," I say.

"You might as well be. You act just like them." He laughs. "I'm not going to write you a ticket. You'd just have Jane throw it out of court. Just keep it safe on the road." He taps the side of the truck with his fist.

I start my engine and contemplate turning around again. Instead, I ease back out toward the Magnolia Mill. Parking, I march to the large open front porch steps. I walk up and down them three times before I finally cop a squat on one of them.

"Did you come here to wear the steps out, or did you come here looking for Jane?" Margret asks from the entryway.

"I don't know what I came here for," I say, honestly.

"You just missed her. She went into town to meet with the councilmen. She's stepping down as mayor."

"What?" I turn my head in her direction. "She loves her job."

"Seems to me she didn't want to face you every day."

"I'll talk to her."

"She's taking over the Magnolia for me. It's gotten to be a bit too much for me trying to raise two babies and being in this dag burn wheelchair."

"One thing I've always admired about you, Margret, is that you've never let those wheels slow you done."

She rolls onto the porch. "And I've never seen a man more in love with a woman walk away from her."

I stand. "It's what's best for the both of us."

"You keep telling yourself that, and you're going to be an awfully lonely man in your aging years. Don't sit back and watch someone else scoop her up. You'll regret it. You should fight harder for her. She's worth it."

"You might be right, but I can't be with a woman who loves two men." I storm to my truck and mutter all the way home, trying to convince myself I'm right to walk away from her.

After pouring a stiff drink, I peel out of my clothes and hit the shower, staying under the spray of the water until it turns cold. I slip on a pair of jeans and pour another drink. My head whips toward the door when I hear a knock. Glancing at my watch, it's near eight, and the sun is starting to set. I guzzle down what's remaining in my glass.

"I know you're in there." Jane's voice is followed by another knock.

CHAPTER TWENTY SIX
JANE

"Y ou ready to leave the hospital? I have the discharge papers in my hand." Wyatt holds them up.

"Yes," I say, sadly, still thinking Ethan will show up.

Wyatt seems to read my mind. "I called him. He's already at work." He escorts me out the door.

We ride in silence on the short drive to the Magnolia. He puts his truck in park and turns in his seat to face me. "Is there anything I can say or do to help you?"

"I'm fine," I sniff. The word fine keeps coming up as if it's a permanent part of my vocabulary.

"Give him some time. He'll come around."

"He needs to stay clear of me." I breathe in,

wincing when I touch my cheek to keep a tear from falling.

"Is that really what you want?"

"It's what's best for him."

"Why do you think so?"

"I have a secret I haven't shared with him."

"We all have secrets, darling." He touches my shoulder.

"This one is big."

"So, you either bury it or tell him."

"If I bury it, I have to walk away from him. It's not the kind of secret you can have between a man and a woman."

"Are you afraid to tell him because you think he'll walk away instead of you?"

I nod and sniff.

"If he truly loves you, it won't matter to him."

"It matters to me, and I hate myself for it." I outright cry on his shoulder.

"Ethan's a good man. He will love you no matter what you tell him."

I pull away from him. "I can't, it's too much, and I won't let him." I jump out of the truck and run into the Magnolia and don't stop until I'm inside my room. I slam my door and press my back to it, dropping to the floor, holding my knees to my chest, sobbing. I sit there until I've run out of tears. I force myself to get up. I'm filthy from the events of last night. Blood stains my shirt, and I suddenly can't stand my clothes next to my skin. I free myself of them, tossing them in the trash. I head to the bathroom and turn on the shower. I turn to face the mirror stark naked. My entire left side of my face is purple and yellow. Four Steri-strips rest under my left eye. My hair is a knotted mess. Brushing it down with my hands, I feel the knot on the back of my head, reminding me of what I went through last night. It doesn't seem real.

Wyatt called the police station and spoke with Mike from my hospital room. With the charges lodged against Matthew, he won't be given bail. I gave my account of the events over the phone, and Mike reassured me he would be locked up for a long time. I can't believe he's the same man I thought at one time I'd spend the rest of my life with. Now the only man I want is Ethan, and he doesn't want me after what happened. What hurts my heart is he didn't give me a chance to explain. Does it really matter, Jane? I ask myself. He deserves a woman who can give him children, not someone who, at any time, could grow ill again.

Stepping into the shower, I let it all wash down the drain. The dirt, the dried blood, and all my feelings. I'll suck it up and move on, get on with my life, alone.

Drying off, I curl up in bed and don't get up for three solid days until I can't stand the banging on my door anymore.

"Enough is a enough! I have a key. I'm coming in!" Margret warns before she opens the door. She maneuvers her wheelchair inside. "You can't keep hiding. It's time to get up and start living," she says, rolling up to the bed. "Good lord, you look awful."

I sit, pulling the sheet over me. "Thanks a lot."

"Your pity party is over. Get out of bed, get dressed and get downstairs. I'm making you breakfast." She aims her wheels toward the door. "Don't make me come back with Wyatt to haul you downstairs," she says over her shoulder.

Who knew Margret could be so gruff. I toss the sheet off, pull some clothes from my closet and walk into the bathroom to brush my teeth. She's right; I look horrid. After slipping my clothes on, I stare in the mirror. The bruising has faded, and the swelling is gone. I wince as I remove the Steri-strips. Washing my face stings. I brush out my knotted hair and pull it back into a pony, then apply makeup, trying to cover what's left of the bruise.

Throwing on shoes, I head downstairs to the

kitchen, where it smells heavenly. My stomach growls in protest of not eating for several days.

"I'm glad to see Wyatt didn't have to pry your naked body out of bed," Margret says, handing me a mug of hot coffee.

I press the cup to my lips and take a sip. "I didn't realize how hungry I was," I say, taking a seat at the breakfast bar.

She sets a plate filled with an omelet and fresh fruit in front of me. "I have pancakes too." She smiles sweetly.

"Thanks for making me get out of bed and for the food." I take in a delicious bite.

"Wyatt and I have a proposition for you." She parks her chair beside me.

"Really. What kind?"

"We want to give you half ownership in the Magnolia Mill."

"What? Why?" I pause my fork midair.

"Because I want to spend more time with my children. You already run this place most days."

"You don't have to give me a stake in this place. I love the time I spend here."

"That's all well and good, but you deserve more, and we want you to have it. You've earned it."

I place my fork down and pick up my coffee, resting back in my chair. If I ran this place full-time,

I'd have to give up my duty as mayor. I wouldn't have to run the risk of seeing Ethan every day. The thought of not seeing him sends an arrow straight to my heart, but it's the break I need to keep arm's length from him. "Can I think about it?"

"Sure you can, but knowing my husband, he's already drawn up an agreement." She wheels over to the sink.

"I won't let you just give it to me. I'll buy half."

"We don't want your money. Besides, you've already earned it."

Nita comes walking through the door, carrying a load of pies. "Here's your order for the week," she says, setting them on the counter.

"You didn't have to carry them over yourself," Margret says.

"I wanted to check on Jane." She turns in my direction. "How are you feeling?"

"I'm fine." There's that word again.

She moves beside me. "We've all been worried about you."

"No need. I'm putting it all behind me." I plaster on a fake smile.

"I'm glad to hear it. You missed our big announcement the other night." She sits.

"Do tell," I say, sipping on my coffee.

"Bear and I are having a baby."

KELLY MOORE

"That's amazing. Congratulations." I hug her and hold back my tears. I'm so happy for the two of them but wish it could be me.

"Thank you. Bear's hoping for a boy."

"I bet Missy is over the moon. How is she, by the way?"

"She's so excited about the baby, I think it was perfect timing to help her. We have her in counseling again, and her therapist seems to think she's working her way through what happened to her."

"Jane has some good news of her own. She's going to be fifty-fifty partners with Wyatt and me in this place."

"That's great," Nita says.

"I haven't agreed to it yet."

"Oh, but you will. You love the Magnolia as much as we do." She grins.

"What about your position as mayor?" Nita asks.

"I'd have to give it up."

"That's a hard decision. You're so good at it, and this town loves you." Nita frowns.

"It might be just what I need right about now."

"Ah, sweetie, don't give up on you and Ethan so easily," Margret says.

"There is no me and Ethan so there's nothing to give up on." I take the last bite of my omelet and walk over to the sink, washing my plate. "I still want a day or two to think about it if you don't mind."

"Take as long as you need," she responds.

"Don't take too long with Ethan, though," Nita adds.

Strolling back over to her, I hug her again. "Congratulations again. Tell Bear I'm happy for him." I bend over, kissing Margret's cheek. "Thanks for bringing me back to reality. I'll give you my answer by the end of the week."

Running back upstairs to my room, I grab my purse and cell phone and I'm plodding into my office in no time.

"It's good to see you back, Jane," my assistant says, laying spreadsheets on my desk.

"Do you know if Mr. York is in his office?"

"He was about an hour ago. Do you want me to call him for you?"

"No, no. I'll go to his office." She leaves, and I get up, staring out my office window for a moment, trying to gather my thoughts. I love him is all that keeps running through my head. I get up the courage to go see him and amble down the long hallway leading to Ethan's office. I hear a woman's voice. It takes me a minute to realize it's Ethan's mother. I press my ear to the door and listen in on their conversation.

. . .

Is there a point to this conversation? Ethan all but yells.

"Wyatt brought her home, and he says she's done nothing but cry," his mother responds.

"And you think I'm responsible for her tears?" I gasp at his words.

"Boone told us what happened."

"Mother, I can't do this with you right now. I have work to do." I hear him snap.

"She loves you." There's a moment of silence.

"And I love her, but I'm not going to be the second man in her heart. I choose to give her up." Tears flood my eyes.

"Oh, so what she wants doesn't really matter."

"You weren't there. I saw the look in her eyes as she pleaded for us not to kill the man who kidnapped her and beat her."

"What are you doing?" I nearly jump out of my skin from Molly's hand on my back.

"What's it look like I'm doing? I'm eavesdropping." I quickly wipe away my tears.

"Why don't you..." I cover her mouth with my hand.

"Keep your voice down." I hush her, moving her away from the door.

"I've been blowing up your phone for days, and this is where I find you? The Jane I know would be marching in there giving Ethan what-for." She crosses her arms over her chest. "Noah told me everything. The Calhoun men were heroes coming after you."

I drag her into my office. "I couldn't agree more." I shut the door.

"Ethan was frantic to find you. Why are you cowering outside his door instead of being in his bed?"

"My actions hurt him. I heard him tell his mother he is 'choosing' to give me up."

"If you'd talk to him, I'm sure you can clear the air with him."

"It's better off left alone." I pace around the room.

"You're speaking nonsense. After what your brother and I went through to be together, there isn't anything the two of you can't overcome." She halts my pacing, placing her hands on my shoulder. "Talk to him."

"I can't." I sigh.

"You're just gonna let him walk away?"

I nod, sucking in my bottom lip.

"You're my best friend, and I love you dearly, but I think you're being foolish."

"You're probably right, but I need to focus on something else right now. Wyatt and Margret have offered me a partnership in the Magnolia."

"What about your job here? I know you've been struggling working part-time at the Mill."

"I think it's best if I resign."

"Hmm..."

"What's that supposed to mean?"

"Nothing." She shrugs. "Are you still planning on going into business with me, or is that out the door too?"

"I'm the silent partner. It won't take time away from my duties at the bed and breakfast."

She grasps her handbag tight over her shoulder. "You should think long and hard before you let a man like Ethan go with all the women in this town salivating to get in his bed."

My mouth falls to the ground. "Nice, Molls, nice."

"I'm just saying."

"Did you come by for a reason?" I say, haughtily.

"Margret told me you were finally out of your room, and I wanted to see about having lunch."

"I appreciate it, but I can't. I'm behind on things here. Tomorrow, I promise."

"I'm going to hold you to it," she says, walking out.

I close the door and buzz Paisley. "Please don't let anyone know I'm here. I have loads of work to catch up on and don't want any distractions."

"Yes, ma'am."

Taking out a pen, I start to work, only to find I've scribbled Ethan's name on my paper. "Damn it. Focus, Jane, focus." I'm my own biggest distraction. The details of the incident with Matthew play out in my head. I shrug them off, then my mind fills with every moment Ethan and I stole together. I cross my legs when I think about the night he spanked me. He gave me something without question, and the hours that followed were glorious.

I find myself biting my bottom lip. The man does love me. He asked me to marry him two times. I know that's not something Ethan takes lightly. Why did I resist him? He and I would be so good together. Wyatt's right. If Ethan loves me, my secret won't matter to him. He's the best thing that's ever happened to me, and I don't want to let him go. I can't imagine the rest of my life without him in it.

I stuff my files in the drawer and grab my bag. I fly back to the Magnolia and change clothes. When I go back downstairs, Margret is trying to contain the twins and take care of the counter.

"I'm so glad you're back. Can you manage the customers through dinner?" She looks frazzled.

I open my mouth to say no, but instead, I put my purse under the counter and dig in. It's so busy that I don't stop until dusk. Wyatt comes in to relieve me.

"I'm sorry you've had to man this alone today. When Margret took the kiddos home, Amelia was running a fever."

"I hope she's alright."

"Doc said she was teething. Nothing serious. I had two cattle birthing, so I couldn't get away."

"It's okay. No need to explain." I clutch my bag and trek toward the front door.

"Where are you going in such an all-fired hurry?"

"I have a secret that needs to be told." I wink at him, and he smiles.

"Good luck," he hollers.

"Thanks. I think I'm going to need it.

CHAPTER TWENTY SEVEN
JANE

Ethan's truck is parked outside his house. I stop my car at Ellie's and get out. I take two things out of my purse; one is my phone, the other I stuff in my pocket. Scanning what I want on my phone, I have it ready for when the time is right.

Padding softly up to the door, I knock and wait for him to answer. As I listen intently, he makes a noise inside. I knock louder this time. "I know you're in there!"

His boots make the floor squeak as he steps across it. The doorknob turns, and Ethan swings it open. Seeing him in blue jeans and a bare chest takes my breath away. My mouth goes dry.

"What do you want, Jane?" he says, gruffly.

"Well, that's a fine how-do-you-do." I try to push by him, but he blocks me.

"Whatever you have to say to me, you can do it from where you stand."

This might be tougher than I thought. "Can we at least sit on the porch step?" I motion the direction with my hand.

He nods, then closes the door behind him.

"You being half naked is very distracting. Can you go put a shirt on?"

"If you insist," he says, disappearing inside.

He comes back with a tight white T-shirt that hugs his pecs. Gah, still distracting. I sit, then he sits.

"I'll ask again, what do you want?"

"The simple answer to your question is you."

He stares at me.

"Did you hear me?"

"I heard you."

"But you don't believe me?"

He shrugs.

"When I was a young, foolish girl, I clung on to the person I thought would make my life better. I didn't realize it at the time, but I used Matthew as much as he did me. I had no idea what love really felt like until you came along. I tried to deny my feelings for you, but they wouldn't go away. I'm thankful

Matthew discarded me, and by no means do I have any feelings left for him."

"Yet, you push me away any chance you get."

"I know I have, but in my mind, I've had my reasons."

"Matthew."

"No!" I swat him in the arm.

We sit in silence for a moment as the sun continues to go down.

He moves to stand. "Nice chat. Let's do it again soon."

I grab his hand. "This isn't going as planned."

He reluctantly sits.

"I love you, Ethan. I'm sorry I haven't been real good at showing it." I rub my hands together. "It's because I've been hiding something from you, and I'm not sure how you're going to react."

He angles toward me. "Are you sick again?" He runs his hand through my hair. "You know it wouldn't change how I feel about you. I'm not a coward like Matthew to turn tail and run."

"Could we not mention his name again?"

"Tell me, Jane."

"I made a choice when I was sick that I will pay for the rest of my life. Had I known I wasn't going to die, I would've chosen differently. I didn't have people lined up to donate a kidney. I thought I wouldn't live past thirty." I look into his eyes, and all I see is love. It gives me the courage to tell him the truth. The truth he deserves. "I can never give you children," I finally blurt out.

He takes his hand off my leg. He'd placed it there as I was talking. I can't get a good read on what he's thinking. "I know you've mentioned several times you wanted kids."

When he looks directly at me, his eyes have misted over. "And you thought I wouldn't want you because you can't have babies?"

I nod, and my tears fall.

He takes my face in both his hands and kisses the spot below my left eye. "I love you, Jane, whether you can have babies or not. We can adopt or not. I don't care as long as I have you."

I kiss him fervently and straddle his lap. "I love you too. I was so afraid you wouldn't want me."

"I want you so badly it fucking hurts," he mutters against my lips. "What do you need me to do to prove it to you?"

"Nothing." I crawl off his lap and get on my knees in front of him. "It's me who needs to prove it to you." I pull out what I placed in my pocket. I show him the palm of my hand. "You said you wouldn't ask me to marry you again, so I'm doing the asking."

He picks up the ring and inspects it. "This is my father's wedding band."

"Yes. Your mother gave it to me a week or so ago. I was going to find you when...a name I won't mention kidnapped me."

He stares at the ring and then at me. "You haven't actually asked me anything."

"I love you, Ethan York. Will you marry me?"

He squints. "No diamonds or flowers?"

I laugh hard, and he hugs me to him, kissing me.

"Wait, I do have something else for you." I take his hand, pulling him off the step. Taking my phone out of my pocket, I hit Play. The night air fills with a sappy country song. "Will you dance with me?"

"Out here in the dirt?"

"Yes."

I hold out my arms, and he joins me under the stars. We sway to the music, holding each other. "You didn't answer the question."

"Which question," he teases, and I smack his ass. "Oh, you want me to spank you again." Even in the dark, I can see the gleam in his eyes.

"Well, yes, but I'm waiting for an answer to my proposal."

He swings me around. "Only if you promise to love me, and no more secrets between us."

"That I can do."

"Then, the answer is yes. I'll marry you, Jane Calhoun."

I step on my tiptoes and devour his mouth. Our tongues mingle as if they were made for one another. His hands roam over my body, landing firmly on my butt as he presses into me. I can feel how turned on he is.

"Do you want to take this dance inside?" I rasp.

He glances down at the ground. "I don't think a little dirt would hurt us."

"We're going to get down and dirty right here, aren't we?" I can't help but smile.

"It's as good a place as any." He chuckles and lowers me to the ground.

It's amazing how fast our clothes fly off. His body covers mine as he slides inside me. I wrap my legs around his muscular ass as he rocks back in forth inside me. "This is how I want it to always be between us," he whispers in my ear.

"I finally get why all the girls' night outs always end with the women going home to their husbands. This is heaven, and there's no place I'd rather be."

SNEAK PEEK AT NEXT BOOK IN
THE SERIES

Whiskey River
Book 7
Whiskey River Road

CHAPTER ONE
CLEM

"Hey, lazybones. You getting up today?" Boone's playful tone has my eyes popping open.

"What time is it?" I yawn and stretch my arms above my head.

"Put it this way, I've already finished my morning work around the ranch, and I'm headed to meet Missy to train her new thoroughbred." He sits on the edge of the bed, changing his boots.

I reach around him, turning the clock in my direction. "It's ten o'clock," I say, jumping out of bed in one move.

Boone chuckles. "You got somewhere to be, doll?"

My head feels woozy, and I take a minute to lean on my dresser.

"You okay?" The bed squeaks when he stands and

walks in my direction, placing his hand on my lower back.

"Yeah. I'm fine. I got up too quickly." I inhale deeply a few times.

"You've been sneaking in a lot of naps lately. Maybe you should let Doc check you out."

Opening a drawer, I pull out a pair of jeans and shimmy into them. "I've got no time for such nonsense. I'm late. I told Winnie I'd cover her pampered pet shop for a couple of hours so she could have an extra-long lunch with Daddy."

"She's got herself a gold mine in the Bark in Style." He sweeps a strand of hair behind my ear. "Are you sure you're okay? You look pale."

"We've just come out of a long, cold winter. A little warm sunshine will perk me right up." I slip a T-shirt over my head with the pet shop logo on the front.

He grabs me around the waist and kisses me sweetly. "Maybe you and I could carve out some time for one another later."

"You say that like we didn't spend hours making love last night." I wipe his lower lip with my thumb.

"After all these years, I still can't get enough of you."

I drape my arms around his neck and give him a proper kiss back.

"Dad! You in there!" Rose pounds on our bedroom door.

"She has terrible timing." I giggle.

"Ignore her. She'll go away." He holds me tighter, deepening our kiss.

"I know you're in there!" She knocks louder.

"I liked her better when she was ten years old." He chuckles.

Our door swings open. "Can I borrow the keys to your truck?" She holds out her hand.

"No," he answers quickly.

"Dad," she whines. "I want to meet my friends at the coffee shop."

"You're too young for coffee." He releases me.

"I'm seventeen. I'm plenty old enough for coffee. Besides, I've been drinking it for years with Grandpa." She puts her hand on her hip like a snarky teenager.

"You're not driving my truck. End of story." He walks out of the bedroom into the living room, and we both follow him.

"All my friends have cars already. When do I get one?"

"When you save enough money to buy one. We've had this conversation repeatedly. You find it more important to spend your money on clothes and make-up." He grabs his Stetson off the hook by the door.

"Your father has offered to help you manage the money you earn."

She dramatically rolls her eyes.

I see Boone hold in a groan.

"I'll drive her. We can finish what we started later." Our lips smack quickly together.

"Do you have to do that kissy stuff in front of me?" Rose's face scrunches up like she smelled something bad.

"I will kiss your mother any time I feel like it," he growls, then heads to his truck.

"Come on. I'm headed to town if you want a ride." I hold the door open.

"Fine," she hisses. She gets in the passenger side of my truck, slamming the door. "Why can't he be like other dads and buy his daughter a car."

"Because he's not like other dads. He wants you to learn responsibility and to take care of the things you buy."

"I need a bigger allowance."

"Then you need to do more chores."

"Mom." She drags out my name.

"You know that's how it works around here. There is plenty to do."

She pouts, glaring out her window.

"You and your dad need to find some common

ground. He's having a hard time with you being a teenager."

"I liked him better when I had him wrapped around my little finger."

"Ha." I laugh. "Believe it or not, you still do. He loves you so much."

A soft smile grows on her face. "I love him too."

"I know you do, sweetie." She turns up the music and sings at the top of her lungs the rest of the way into town. She hops out as soon as I park in front of the pet store.

"Text me when you need a ride home," I call after her. She waves and runs down the block to meet her friends at the coffee shop.

I walk up the cute pathway leading to the shop. The Closed sign is flipped over, but when I push the door, it opens. "That's strange." No one is behind the counter. "Hello," I say, walking into the back office. I hear noise coming from one of the storage rooms. I'm frightened when I see a chair toppled over and a box lying upside down on the floor. I dig my revolver out of my purse. My hand shakes as I turn the door-knob. I swing it open quickly, hoping to catch whoever is in there off guard.

"Oh my gawd! Daddy!" I cover my eyes with my hand. "I'm gonna have to bleach my eyeballs out to erase this picture from my mind."

"Why don't you try knocking before you come barreling inside," he grumbles, hiking up his pants.

"I thought you flipped the sign to Closed," Winnie whispers to him.

"I did. Evidently, my daughter can't read." She wipes the lipstick from Daddy's cheek.

"You two act like a couple of horny teenagers. Can't you keep your shenanigans to your house?"

"Do you know how many times over the years I've caught my children doing their hanky-panky in the barn?" He pushes by me. "Besides, I ain't wasting one of those blue pills doc gave me to try."

"I'm so sorry, Clem," Winnie says, straightening her blouse.

"Don't you be apologizing to her," he huffs.

"I appreciate you working for a few hours." Her face is flushed.

"It's no problem at all, minus seeing my daddy's white ass in the air."

"You just wait until you're my age." He points at me.

"Are you two ever tying the knot?" I ask.

"We're happy with the way things are, dear." She smiles.

"I keep trying to get her to marry me, but she has it in that thick skull of hers that we should keep our finances separate."

She takes my hand in hers. "I don't want to have any claims to Whiskey River Ranch. Your daddy has built the place from the ground up, and all the Calhouns have put their blood, sweat, and tears into the land. It belongs to each of you, not me."

"She still wants me to charge her rent, for god's sake," he snaps.

"I'm not getting in the middle of this." I turn toward Winnie. "You and Ethan are family."

Scar barks twice when she comes into the room. Daddy bends down, picking her up. "Some watchdog you are." He strokes her furless body.

"I have a seller dropping off two Labrador puppies at noon. There is a check in the top drawer of my desk." She points.

"I'll take care of it. You two enjoy your lunch together but for Pete's sake, Daddy, keep your britches on." I laugh.

"Would you like us to bring you back something to eat?" Winnie takes his hand to walk him out.

"Jane is stopping by with Nita's special of the day."

"Good. I've been worried about you. You've lost weight," she states.

"That's what having a teenage daughter does to you. She keeps me so busy, I forget to eat." Truth be known, I've not had an appetite. Perhaps Boone is right; I should get a checkup. I can't remember the last time I had a physical.

"Here." Daddy hands me Scar.

"We'll be gone for a couple hours." He kisses my cheek.

"I'll take care of things, don't worry."

I walk to them to the front door. Daddy winks at Winnie when he flips over the Open sign.

Several customers walk in at the same time. I'm always surprised by how busy the store is. I didn't think Salt Lick had a need for a fancy froufrou pet store, but her customers love it.

The bell above the door jingles and Ethan and Jane walk in hand in hand. "Hey, Clem. Have you seen Molly? She and Noah are supposed to meet us here."

"Not yet."

Ethan hands me a white bag with a Styrofoam box. "I was tempted to eat it on my way over. It smells delicious."

My stomach rolls. "Excuse me," I say, running for the bathroom. I make it just in time to release the contents of my stomach into the toilet. I heave several times, then wash my face with cool water. Boone's right. I am pale. I inhale deeply and head back into the shop.

"You alright?" Ethan looks concerned.

"Yeah, I'm fine. I think I have a stomach bug or something."

"Do you want us to cover for you here so you can go home?"

"Don't be silly. I'll be fine."

The door jingles again, and it's Molly and Noah, with their new baby Blaise tucked in her arms, and their two-year-old Eden, clinging to Noah's leg.

"They are so adorable," I say.

Jane takes Blaise from Molly's arms. Jane spoils all her nieces and nephews rotten.

"Where are all of you headed?" I ask.

"We're going to pick blackberries and have a picnic down by the river. Ellie and her kiddos are joining us," Molly says.

"What about Ian?" I ask.

"He's out of town working on blueprints for a new resident of Salt Lick," Noah responds.

"Ellie must have her hands full with the three kids."

"She does. It will be good for them to play with their cousins," Jane says.

"You guys have fun," I say, shooing them out the door.

The store isn't empty long. Customers come and go. I see a man carrying a kennel with two pups inside. I hold open the door for him to enter.

"These must be the two dogs Winnie was telling me about."

"They are my son's dogs. Mrs. York said she'd buy them from me and find them a good home."

"Put the kennel over there, and I'll go get you the check she left for you."

"Thank you."

I run to the back and find the check right where she said it would be. I give it to him, and he leaves. I get on the floor to look at the two chocolate-colored puppies. "You two are so cute. I think I know two teenage girls that would love to get their hands on you." They lick my fingers through the metal door of the kennel.

Missy has been begging Bear and Nita to get her and Walker a dog. They wanted to wait until their son was older. I think six is old enough. Rose will want one simply because Missy will have one. Those two have been inseparable since the day Rose moved in with us. I'm glad they are so close. They're more like sisters than cousins.

"Who do you have there?" I didn't see Boone come into the shop.

"Hey. What are you doing here?"

"I thought I'd see if Rose needed a ride home."

"How sweet of you." I stand on my tiptoes, kissing his short beard.

"I might have been a little hard on her. I want to teach her to drive my truck."

"Oh, she'll love that."

"The way you were looking at those two when I walked in, I'm assuming we'll have two new dogs at Whiskey River."

"Bear's been promising Missy a dog."

"Which means the other one is Rose's." He chuckles.

"Are you okay with that?"

"Whatever makes you happy, doll. Have you had lunch yet?"

My hand automatically covers my stomach. "Jane brought food, but I'm just not hungry."

He feels my forehead. "I wish you'd see the doctor."

"I'll make an appointment."

"Thank you." He looks around the store. "We could slip in the back room." He waggles his eyebrows.

"Not on your life," I roar. "I caught my daddy and Winnie spanking uglies in the storage closet. It was plumb awful seeing his ass in the air."

He laughs. "Go Chet. The old man still has it in him."

"You ain't right. That's my father you're rooting on." I playfully swat him in the chest.

"He's still a man, in love with a woman."

"I like that he and Winnie are together. She's good for him."

"He's a happy man."

A few more customers walk through the door. "I need to mind the store. You go find Rose."

"I'll load these two into the back of my truck." He picks up the kennel.

"Okay. I'll see you at home later."

"Call the doctor," he urges.

"I will. I will. I promise."

ABOUT THE AUTHOR

"This author has the magical ability to take an already strong and interesting plot and add so many unexpected twists and turns that it turns her books into a complete addiction for the reader." Dandelion Inspired Blog

Signup for Newsletter

Armed with books in the crook of my elbow, I can go anywhere. That's my philosophy! Better yet, I'll write the books that will take me on an adventure.

My heroes are a bit broken but will make you swoon. My heroines are their own kick-ass characters armed with humor and a plethora of sarcasm.

If I'm not tucked away in my writing den, with coffee firmly gripped in hand, you can find me with a book propped on my pillow, a pit bull lying across my legs, a Lab on the floor next to me, and two kittens running amuck.

My current adventure has me living in Idaho with my own gray-bearded hero, who's put up with my shenanigans for over thirty years, and he doesn't mind all my book boyfriends.

If you love romance, suspense, military men, lots of action and adventure infused with emotion, tear-worthy moments, and laugh-out-loud humor, dive into my books and let the world fall away at your feet.

ALSO BY KELLY MOORE

Whiskey River Road Series - Available on Audible

Coming Home, Book 1

Stolen Hearts, Book 2

Three Words, Book 3

Kentucky Rain, Book 4

Wild Ride, Book 5

Magnolia Mill, Book 6

The Broken Pieces Series in order

Broken Pieces

Pieced Together

Piece by Piece

Pieces of Gray

Syn's Broken Journey

Broken Pieces Box set Books 1-3

August Series in Order

Next August

This August

Seeing Sam

The Hitman Series- Previously Taking Down Brooklyn/The DC Seres

Stand By Me - On Audible as Deadly Cures

Stay With Me On Audible as Dangerous Captive

Hold Onto Me

Epic Love Stories Series can be read in any order

Say You Won't Let Go. Audiobook version

Fading Into Nothing Audiobook version

Life Goes On. Audiobook version

Gypsy Audiobook version

Jameson Wilde Audiobook version

Rescue Missions Series can be read in any order

Imperfect. On Audible

Blind Revenge

Fated Lives Series

Rebel's Retribution Books 1-4. Audible

Theo's Retaliation Books 5-7. Audible

Thorn's Redemption Audible

Fallon's Revenge Book 11 Audible

The Crazy Rich Davenports Season One in order of reading

The Davenports On Audible

Lucy

Yaya

Ford

Gemma

Daisy

The Wedding

Halloween Party

Bang Bang

Coffee Tea or Me